"You should do th

"What?" Jack asked.

"Laugh. Your whole face seems to light up and you don't look so miserable."

There was that word again. *Miserable.* Rachel seemed to have honed in on it for some reason.

"I'll make a mental note," he assured her.

Rachel made her way toward the other doorway from the dining room that led back into the foyer. He followed behind, not too close, but close enough to get some floral notes from her perfume or lotion.

"Thanks for coming by," he stated, reaching around to open the door for her. "I really do value this friendship we have."

Rachel tossed a glance over her shoulder and held him in place with that piercing stare. "Are we friends?"

Well, now he felt ridiculous if she was questioning him.

"I thought—"

"I'm teasing." She grinned. "So, since we're friends, I'll be sure to let Mama know you'll be coming for dinner soon. Good night, Jack."

She patted his cheek and headed out onto the wide porch, disappearing into the night.

Looks like he was going to a family dinner.

Julia Ruth is a *USA TODAY* bestselling author, married to her high school sweetheart and values her faith and family above all else. Julia and her husband have two teen girls and they enjoy their beach trips, where they can unwind and get back to basics. Since she grew up in a small rural community, Julia loves keeping her settings in fictitious towns that make her readers feel like they're home. You can find Julia on Instagram: juliaruthbooks.

Books by Julia Ruth

Love Inspired

Four Sisters Ranch

A Cowgirl's Homecoming
The Cowboy's Inheritance

Visit the Author Profile page at LoveInspired.com.

The Cowboy's Inheritance

JULIA RUTH

LOVE INSPIRED
INSPIRATIONAL ROMANCE

LOVE INSPIRED®

INSPIRATIONAL ROMANCE

ISBN-13: 978-1-335-93681-3

The Cowboy's Inheritance

Copyright © 2024 by Julia Bennett

Recycling programs for this product may not exist in your area.

This is a work of fiction. Names, characters, places and incidents are either the product of the author's imagination or are used fictitiously. Any resemblance to actual persons, living or dead, businesses, companies, events or locales is entirely coincidental.

For questions and comments about the quality of this book, please contact us at CustomerService@Harlequin.com.

® is a trademark of Harlequin Enterprises ULC.

Love Inspired
22 Adelaide St. West, 41st Floor
Toronto, Ontario M5H 4E3, Canada
www.LoveInspired.com

Printed in Lithuania

MIX
Paper | Supporting responsible forestry
FSC® C021394

Rejoicing in hope; patient in tribulation;
continuing instant in prayer.
—*Romans* 12:12

Grace and Madelyn, I hope you both always set the biggest goals, let nothing stand in your way and pray with each step you take.

Chapter One

Rachel Spencer tightened her grip on the reins as she brought Sunshine to a halt. She adjusted the wide brim of her hat to block the bright morning sun from her eyes. She still couldn't quite see who had pulled into the Circle H Ranch twenty minutes ago, but whoever drove that sporty black car evidently wanted to stick out like the proverbial sore thumb. No one in Rosewood Valley cared about money, let alone flashing their material possessions around.

Was this person the new owner of the neighboring ranch? A ribbon of remorse curled through her gut, both at the loss of her beloved neighbor and the potential loss of this prime piece of land. Oh, she had no money to purchase, but surely there was something she could do, right? She didn't believe she'd come this far and jumped every hurdle life had thrown at her to just miss her dream property. Besides, anyone who drove something so sporty and ostentatious likely had no clue how to properly care for a farm. Probably had shiny shoes that wouldn't dare go near a cow field or a chicken coop.

Rachel glanced at her own worn cowgirl boots as she pushed her bitterness aside. With a tap of her heel to Sunshine's flank, she started forward again. She had to get a closer look. She wasn't sure what her intent had been when she saddled up in her family's barn moments ago, but the unknown had been eating at her since she'd seen the sports car speeding down the two-lane road right past Four Sisters Ranch this morning.

If nothing else, she needed to introduce herself and give a stern warning about the tractors that were often on the road.

She truly wished her mood would lift, but she was human and lately there seemed to be one blow after another. She really wanted to catch a break.

Rachel actually wondered if she should turn back and not come across as some nosy town crier ready to spread the word on the newbie. In a town this small, she'd have no problem finding out what was going on with George Hart's property and who this stranger was.

But just as she had the thought to leave, a tall man came around from the side of the wraparound porch. He adjusted his dark sunglasses, then propped his hands on his hips as he stared out onto the front yard. The jeans and simple T-shirt didn't seem flashy, which was quite a juxtaposition to the black car sitting in the drive. But then she squinted to his shoes... Yup, shiny. Just like the car.

Sunshine let out a neigh and the stranger on the porch jerked his attention her way. So much for sneaking in and out.

"Thanks a lot," she muttered to her mare.

With another soft tap to her side, Sunshine took a casual approach across the field and onto the Circle H. Raking her gaze over the pristine two-story white farmhouse sent a warmth through Rachel. This was the exact type of home she'd always envisioned for herself and the family she wanted someday. Flower boxes under each window and a porch with swings and rocking chairs that just begged for family gatherings and sweet tea on a summer day. At least, that was how she dreamed of her future.

"Mornin'," she called.

No reply in return. The man remained still and didn't seem to get the memo that folks around here were chatty and friendly. Well, if he had any intention of sticking around, he'd have to learn real quick.

Considering she'd much rather figure out who this handsome stranger was than get back to her term paper due at the end of the week for her online class, she kicked Sunshine back into gear.

"You're new here."

Way to state the obvious.

"I'm Rachel Spencer," she added so he didn't think she was completely crazy. "From Four Sisters Ranch."

"Jack."

Rachel waited, but apparently "just Jack" had no last name. Regardless of his lack of manners and social skills, she smiled. Maybe she could get him to crack a smile as well. Not that he wasn't handsome enough with that light sandy hair and dark brown eyes. Even from on top of her horse, Jack seemed tall, over six feet, if she was guessing.

"I take it you're the new owner," she said.

"Something like that."

Rachel held on to the reins as she threw her leg over the saddle and dismounted. She led her mare closer to the porch as she tried to squelch her worries and her curiosity. If desperation and adoration could buy this land, she would have already signed her name on the deed long ago.

Being nearly thirty-five and living in a loft apartment over a barn on your parents' property seemed a little pathetic and unstable. Not to mention her parents needed that extra space for their growing farm-to-table events business they'd launched just a few months ago. Who knew offering such an experience would be such a huge success?

Her sister Jenn, that was who. The brainchild behind the operation.

Rachel knew her parents would never ask her to leave and would never even hint that they needed the space, but considering she knew the ins and outs of the daily operation—not only with the farm, but also all the growing events they'd added to bring in more income—it was well past time she move on and start her own legacy... and the Circle H was the perfect place.

Now, if she could only figure out how to buy when the bank had approved her for a certain amount and this place was worth well beyond that, no doubt... If it even went up for sale. Which was why she had to be careful in her questioning but still figure out the intentions of this stranger.

"You need any help settling in?" she offered. "My mother will likely bake something to welcome you to the neighborhood, but I'm more of a hands-on girl, if you and your wife need any help moving things."

Jack came down the steps and stood at the base. Now that they were on even ground, she could appreciate his height and broad shoulders. The lean frame and heavy-lidded stare shouldn't have her heart beating faster, but she was human and couldn't help how she felt. He had that city vibe with his polished attire, but a bit of his messy hair made him seem just a bit country, like he'd just removed his hat.

She'd never ogled another woman's husband before. She really should have turned around earlier when she had the chance. Yet here she was, unable to move her feet.

"It's just me and I won't be staying here for long," he explained.

Something about that statement both pleased and intrigued her, but she couldn't take the time to assess all her thoughts. She'd crossed property lines on a mission.

"Putting the farm on the market?" she asked, wondering if she could get some type of ballpark price to see exactly what she was working with so she could start praying.

"Soon."

A blossom of hope opened and she took a step forward. "I've always loved this place," she told him. "As a little girl I'd come visit and maybe make a pest of myself." She smiled thinking of the summer afternoons she'd spent here with her sisters. Come to think of it, one of the reasons they'd spent so many summer days here was because of their neighbor's grandson, an older boy who'd captured their interest. She chuckled as she recalled. "George Hart had the cutest grandson that would visit from out of town. I might have had a little crush, though now I can't even recall his name. I showed him how to bait a hook to fish on the pond in the back. He was absolutely terrible at fishing."

Rachel laughed and shook her head at the adolescent recollection, realizing she'd been babbling. "Sorry. I just have so many memories of this place. So, how did you know the owner?"

Jack took two slow, easy steps and stood just a few feet from her when a crooked, adorable smile spread across his face. She'd been waiting on a smile from him, but now that he presented it, she had a pit in her stomach because he looked a bit like he knew something she didn't.

"I'm the grandson and terrible fisherman."

* * *

Rachel. Her infectious grin faltered just enough to know she regretted her words, but her childhood secret hovered between them now.

He remembered the infamous four sisters hanging around, but it had always been Rachel who wanted to fish in the pond and help on the farm. She'd been such a tomboy, and from the looks of it, not much had changed. Her long hair fell in a braid over one slender shoulder and her white cowgirl hat shielded her eyes. Her worn jeans, even more worn boots and simple red T-shirt were all perfect staples of the girl-next-door look. Quite the opposite of the women he was used to seeing back in San Francisco. Many of them preferred heels to boots and makeup over a natural look. He had to admit, Rachel was nice to look at.

"Is this when I turn and leave and we pretend I didn't just admit my ten-year-old crush on you?"

Yeah. Quite different. Bold and assertive right off the bat. Something about that confused him. He wasn't used to women like that, but the other part of him found her intriguing and refreshing. The last woman he'd gone on a date with had giggled her way through the evening, almost trying too hard to give him attention.

Not that he was looking for a love connection—he was looking for a buyer. He had one goal in mind—to sell his grandfather's farmhouse quickly and figure out what to do with the feed store in town that had also been willed to him. Then get back to San Francisco. Finding a date wasn't even on the page of his to-do list. Gaining his father's approval and taking over the new real estate office came above all else. He hadn't worked this hard to prove himself to his only living family member just to lose this promotion to a guy who wasn't even family…but acted like the son Jack's father had always wanted.

Forget about Brian.

"No need to leave," Jack stated, concentrating on the here and now. "You're the only person I halfway know in this town."

He might be solely focused on his business goals, but that didn't mean he wanted to purposely embarrass her, either. Even though he'd been raised by a single father driven by money and a career, Jack still had loving nannies who'd taught him manners, morals and how to respect women.

"I'm sure my parents will remember you." She tipped her head and pursed her lips just enough to draw his attention to her unpainted mouth. "I'm not sure you'd recall them, though. Will and Sarah Spencer. Dad rarely leaves the farm, but I know my mother came over and brought food and canned goods."

Jack tried to recollect, but those summers were a blur. He did remember a few times going over to the farm next door and the girls always being around. But mostly when Jack thought back to that time, all he remembered was being happy and content and…loved. His grandfather always tried to get his work done while entertaining a growing, curious boy who knew absolutely nothing about farming. Jack wouldn't remember a thing he'd been taught, so by the time the next summer visit rolled around, he'd have to learn all over again.

Being back now, well…he hadn't expected such a punch of nostalgia. He didn't think the place would have so much feeling, especially with his grandfather not here. Jack had been so conflicted with emotions and guilt when his grandfather passed, he'd not come back for the funeral. He hadn't seen his grandfather in so long because Jack had let his life get in the way, he'd felt like he didn't deserve to mourn with all those from the town who loved him.

But now he was back, and everywhere he looked, Jack saw the man who'd helped shape his life. From the fence by the barn Jack helped his grandfather nail into place, to the old porch swing where they'd share a cold glass of lemonade after a hard day's work.

He'd known many hard days in the real estate grind. And he didn't know what he'd do if he didn't get that promotion. Out of all the deals he'd had in his career, this was the biggest. His next move up the ladder hinged on this one sale and how much he'd get from the property...the property his grandfather had willed to him, completely bypassing Jack's father.

There was no plan B if he didn't sell this for top dollar. It was time he had his own office with his own staff and his own way of running the family real estate company.

"So, why sell?" Rachel asked, pulling him from his thoughts. "Not that it's my business, but this place is amazing."

"For some," he agreed. "But my home is in San Francisco."

"City boy."

"Through and through," he confirmed.

She snickered. "The shoes and the car were dead giveaways."

He wasn't sure if that was a dig or merely an observation. He'd worked hard for his things. That didn't mean he wasn't thankful, but he wouldn't be sorry. Maybe sometimes his taste leaned on the expensive side, but he had no other responsibilities other than to himself, so what was he hurting?

"What will you be asking for the farm?" she asked.

Was she interested? Or knew someone who was? "Why? You have a buyer?"

"I need a place and I've always loved this property." Rachel shrugged, then adjusted her hat. "Depends on the price."

"All cash is preferable and I'd like to have this closed within thirty days once I get it on the market," he told her before throwing out a ballpark range. "I suppose I could wait on someone to get a loan so long as there's no set-backs."

Her brows rose as her shoulders fell, and the only word he could use to describe her would be *defeated*. Clearly she was hoping for something else, but he was here for business and that was all he knew.

"Thirty days is short," she finally replied. "Why the rush?"

Jack slid his hands into his pockets. "I don't really have a reason to stay here and I don't need a farm." No reason to keep up this property now that his grandfather was gone. Using this piece of land was the fastest, not to mention only, way to gain access to a portion of the family company, which he and Brian were neck and neck for. His father had pretty much stated this would be his best chance for success. "I'd like a quick, easy sale so I can get back to my life."

Rachel squared her shoulders and tipped her chin as she held his gaze. "I'm sure we can work something out. I fully intend to make sure I'm the new owner of the Circle H before you leave town."

If he thought she seemed defeated earlier, she had the look of a very determined woman now. But that grit staring back told him she didn't have the means to make this place hers, so his time here in Rosewood Valley was about to get very interesting.

Chapter Two

Rachel had called herself all kinds of a fool for the past twenty-four hours. What on earth had she been thinking blurting out such a bold, confident statement to Jack about the Circle H yesterday?

She hadn't been thinking, and that was how she found herself in an extremely awkward situation. One she couldn't stop mulling over as she drove into town to run errands. She only hoped Jack wouldn't be at his grandfather's store today and that she could avoid him a little longer. She just never learned her lesson. Her mouth often got her in trouble, but when she was passionate about something, sometimes her thoughts and words overrode her common sense.

As the oldest of four, Rachel had always let her words spill out before she truly thought everything through. Like the time she told her father she would take his early morning barn chores over the summer before her sixteenth birthday if he'd consider buying her a truck. About day three of that summer, she'd started wondering why she ever tossed out such a proposal. But that was when she truly started to appreciate the work of a farmer.

She'd really put her foot in her mouth this time. That daring, definite statement she'd left with Jack dropped a heavy weight of dread in her gut. Oh, sure, she wanted nothing more than to hand over an all-cash offer and move into that house today, but the harsh reality was she wasn't there financially. She didn't know if she ever would be, but she had every intention of trying and refused to back down.

Which was why she'd secretly enrolled in online schooling. Her business degree with an emphasis in agriculture would help her in the future. She wanted to assist young farmers or new ranchers to the area in getting a start and making smart decisions.

Now she just needed to take her own advice about said smart decisions and think before she spoke. More than that, though, she needed to pray. Relying on her own devices wouldn't get her very far in life, and she'd been taught at an early age to pray over anything and everything.

She'd prayed for her own ranch, her own future. She'd prayed for God to send the right man so she could start her family and begin making memories of the life she'd always envisioned. God's timing was always going to be better than her own... At least, that was what her father always told her. She just didn't know how long she'd have to wait to find that happy ending.

Rachel pulled into the lot of the All Good Things Feed Store and tried to focus on her mission today and not her unsettled nerves. She had offered to go get the grains for the horses today, since her mom had finagled her dad into hanging new curtains in the guest bedrooms. She needed the ride into town to clear her head anyway, but now that she was here, she was no more relaxed.

On a sigh, Rachel grabbed her purse and stepped from her truck. She adjusted her braid over her shoulder and smiled at a patron heading from the old two-story barn turned feed store. A variety of potted plants and hanging baskets decorated the front entrance in a nice display that she knew for a fact the new hire, Emily, had handled. That girl had a green thumb and a love for animals. And that was the type of person Rachel hoped to help with her degree when the time came.

As soon as she stepped through the wide-open doors that allowed fresh summer air to waft through, that familiar scent of grain and hay hit her. She loved the country life and couldn't imagine any other way of living. Rosewood Valley and all its simplicity and beauty would always be home. The way the little town was nestled between the rolling hills of Northern California, the white church surrounded by lush evergreens, and the farms that made up her community would always make her smile. She wanted nothing more than to build the next stage of her life here; she just prayed that would happen soon. She knew she had to trust God's timing, but still, she had human feelings and emotions and wanted to speed things along. With her sister Jenn engaged and getting married soon, that only made Rachel wish for her own true love to come along.

"But the grains and vegetables would be best, from everything I've seen online."

The worried tone had Rachel glancing at the lady standing at the checkout counter. She tried not to eavesdrop as she began to get her own things, but it was impossible not to overhear. She didn't know who sounded more panicked, the customer or the worker Rachel didn't recognize…which meant he was fairly new. Her father typically did the feed store runs, and Rachel hadn't been in for quite some time.

She checked out the endcap with its fresh supply of vitamins and figured her own homemade holistic options were still better for her family's livestock. She always supported the local store and bought what they needed for the farm, but she also integrated some of her own all-natural herbs. She continued to survey the stock, all the while listening to the duo behind her, who both seemed extremely confused.

"I've only been here a few months, ma'am," the young worker stated. "I'm not sure on that type of supplement, though."

"Is there anyone here who is?" the patron asked.

"I'm afraid they don't come in until this afternoon, but I can call someone else if you need an answer right now. Our manager is on vacation until next week."

Rachel spun around. "I'm sorry," she intervened before she could stop herself. "I couldn't help but hear that you need guidance with some chicken supplements. I can offer my opinion if you don't mind."

The middle-aged woman's shoulders relaxed as she smiled. "Please. I've never had chickens, and my granddaughter talked me into getting some. I can't kill them already and I'm worried I'll feed them the wrong things. I've seen so many suggestions online."

Rachel returned the lady's smile and took a step forward. "I've grown up around chickens, and to be honest, there are some great at-home remedies you can supplement into the feed options you'll find here. Depending on the type of chickens you have, they can generally eat it if humans can. If that makes sense."

She didn't want to take business from the store, but she also felt that being honest about things she had at home was another great way to ensure trust in any customer. Rachel went on to explain some basic spices and pantry items the woman could use for the chickens to keep them healthy.

"The key with chickens is to start doing these things to prevent any illness from coming on in the first place," Rachel added. "They're pretty easy creatures once you get the hang of it."

"Well, that's reassuring." The lady laughed. "Since my granddaughter came to live with me, she's been begging for chickens so she can get eggs, and I bought some before thinking through the actual day-to-day care."

"I can definitely understand rash decisions." Rachel sighed. Boy, did she ever. "But you'll be just fine and the people here are always so helpful."

"Sorry about that," the new worker chimed in. "I'm still learning."

Rachel waved her hand. "No worries. Everyone has to start somewhere and you're trying. You'll get the hang of things in no time. I'm Rachel Spencer, by the way."

She held out her hand and the teen shook it. "Myles Taylor," he replied.

"Myles, my family is in here nearly every day, so you'll be seeing quite a bit of us. My father is Will Spencer."

The young boy's brows drew together. "Red suspenders?"

Rachel laughed at her father's well-known signature style. "That's him."

She took a step back and turned her attention to the customer. "Sorry I interrupted. Just thought I'd give some input from my years with chickens."

The woman nodded. "I'm quite glad you did."

Rachel offered her another smile before she turned back around. She caught someone at the end of an aisle moving away and out of sight. She didn't quite see a face, but she'd recognize those fancy shoes anywhere. Someone needed a pair of cowboy boots if he didn't want to stand out like a city slicker.

* * *

Jack made his way back to the feed store office as discreetly as possible. He'd stared at financial statements and backed-up bills all morning and they just weren't making sense. He'd decided to head out onto the floor to look at the layout and get a feel for things so he could give his eyes a break from all the disturbing numbers.

Then he'd heard that familiar voice. The woman who claimed she'd be buying his grandfather's farm. The adorable neighbor who had wide green eyes and a soft smile and a bold attitude that intrigued him more than it should.

Apparently she had to step in and assist a customer, and she did so in such a graceful way that she didn't embarrass the new hire. He shouldn't find every single trait about her so attractive—that certainly wasn't why he'd come to town—but he couldn't help himself. Jack shuffled through more files. Who in the world kept so many paper records, anyway?

Rosewood Valley truly was slow-paced and laid-back, almost in a different era. There were probably still pay phones on the corners.

"I thought that was you."

Jack dropped the stack of statements and glanced over his shoulder. Rachel leaned against the door frame and looped one of her thumbs through her belt loops. Long strands of dark and light brown hair intertwined in a braid that fell over one shoulder. She held on to the brim of her hat in her free hand as she met his gaze.

"How did you know I was here?" he asked.

She gestured her hat toward his shoes. "You're really going to need to change those if you want to blend in. What are you doing at the store today?"

He sighed and turned to ease a hip on the edge of the

desk. "I figure I needed to see my other inheritance from Grandpa. I got here early and introduced myself to Myles. Good kid. Needs to learn more about the store, though."

"He will. He's nervous. Does he know who you are?"

Jack nodded. "I told him my grandfather owned the place and I'm in town to settle his affairs. I also told him I know nothing about a feed store, so thankfully you came in when you did, because I know as much about feeding chickens as I do about winning the Super Bowl."

"Happy to help," she replied with a wide grin. "I know a few new people have been hired lately, so there might be some growing pains until they all learn the ropes."

He wasn't sure there was enough time to get through everyone learning the ropes if these numbers kept declining. He'd need to talk to the manager, but the guy was out for a week on vacation. Jack didn't believe the books looked right, but he really didn't know what to think. He knew he had to be careful about how he handled this situation. Not only because he didn't want gossip spreading, but also because Jack was an outsider coming into this small town. He wanted to honor his grandfather's legacy and not leave a dark stain or tarnish George Hart's reputation in any way. His grandfather had impeccable character and Jack intended to protect that.

Though Jack had to wonder why the store and the farm hadn't gone to his father. Jack figured his grandpa knew that out of the two familial options, Jack would be the one to take the most care and do the right thing. His father never wanted anything to do with this lifestyle. Jack didn't either, but he had more of an emotional connection.

So here he sat with a bustling small-town store and a farm, and he had no idea how to run either. The farm would be sold to someone who could handle it. As for the feed store, his father hadn't insisted he sell that, so Jack was still on the fence. Maybe he'd keep this as an investment property.

"Something wrong?"

Rachel straightened from the doorway and took one step in. There wasn't much room, so he shifted around to the other side of the desk so they weren't so cramped.

"I'm not sure, honestly." He sighed, glancing down at the stack of papers. He needed to focus and not second-guess his grandfather's intentions or reasoning. "I'm a numbers guy and nothing here is adding up. Literally. It's quite a mess."

Rachel set her hat on the edge of the desk and picked up one of the statements. Jack waited while her bright eyes scanned the document. She looked from that paper to the desk, then back to him. The worry lines between her brows creased.

"Not a lot of money in this one," she murmured. "I'm sure he had other accounts."

"The other accounts are overdrawn."

Rachel's eyes widened. "What? That's just… That's not right."

"No, it's not. His name is on the account as well as the manager's."

"Walt is a trustworthy man." Rachel set the paper back on top of the others. "I've known him almost as long as I knew your grandfather. He wouldn't do anything shady, if that's what you're thinking."

"I really don't know what I'm thinking, but I don't know the guy. Until I can talk to him, I'm not sure what to do. I'd like someone to do some investigating and check things out around here. I guess I can hang around and act like I want to see the ins and outs."

Rachel's lips quirked. "And what will you do when someone asks you a question about worming medications or that their horse has a cough?"

Yeah, he hadn't thought about any of that. He only knew he needed to see if how much was coming in was actually coming in.

"I might have to stay here in the office for the most part," he amended. "The credit card receipts and the cash in aren't matching up. I feel like I need a set of eyes and ears, and I have no idea who to trust."

"No problem," she piped up. "I'll do it."

Jack jerked back slightly. "You'll do what?"

"I'll hang around the store, help customers, be discreet to see if anything weird is going on. That way when Walt gets back, he won't think anything and you won't be lurking over everyone's shoulder in your fancy shoes."

He had no clue why she was so hung up on his shoes, but he couldn't worry or think about that right now. He needed to concentrate on getting the house ready to sell and getting top dollar. He certainly hadn't expected to run into a snag at the feed store.

"Why would you offer to do this?" Jack asked, crossing his arms over his chest. "You want something in return?"

She shrugged one slender shoulder. "I would never do something for someone and expect a favor in return, but I think we could help each other for the time being."

Intrigued, he shifted his stance and leveled his gaze. The young tomboy he recalled had grown into a striking, intriguing woman who seemed to know her work and was passionate about this lifestyle. Not to mention she had a smart business mind, which was definitely something he could appreciate. Negotiations were very much in his wheelhouse, so she had his undivided attention.

"For reasons I don't want to get into, I need the money, so I'd need this to be a paid position," she added.

"Fair enough," he replied. Even though the place was in a financial disaster, if she could fix this issue, she'd be invaluable. "What else?"

"I'm sure you'll want to renovate the farmhouse, but I hope your ideas aren't too…"

He waited while she seemed to struggle with the right word. She twisted her hands together and pursed her lips, which amused him.

"Just say it," he coerced. "You won't hurt my feelings."

"Flashy."

She kept using that term to describe him, and he'd never had anyone say that before. He didn't think his style was over-the-top, but he wasn't here for a makeover of any kind, so her thoughts didn't matter—at least, not about his fashion sense.

"So I think I should help you with your renovations." She dropped her hands at her sides and shrugged. "I also want a chance at first dibs when you get done and decide to sell. Maybe we can work something out as far as a lease to own or something like that."

Jack hadn't seen that coming. Lease to own? There was simply no way. He had to sell—and at top dollar so he could get that promotion and get back to San Francisco.

"I can't do those terms," he replied. "The farm will have to be a straight sale, no lease or rent or land contracts."

That smile on her face faltered slightly, but she composed herself in seconds. With her chin tipped like he'd seen her do just yesterday, she quirked a dark brow.

"I would think that what I can bring to not only the farm but also this feed store would be worth your time to consider my proposal." She tossed out a number for her wages that he deemed fair before she went on. "I can start here tomorrow and I'll keep our communication line open. I'm sure once you see what I offer, you might just work with me on that property after all."

And with that parting statement, she tapped the brim of her hat and turned, walking out of his office like she hadn't heard his refusal. Clearly this woman knew what she wanted and didn't take no for an answer once she set her sights on something.

Which left Jack wondering if he found that annoying or surprisingly more attractive.

Chapter Three

❧

"Have you found a buyer yet?"

Jack made his way from the back porch of the farmhouse and down the stone path toward the guesthouse. He'd been making more notes of renovation ideas when his father called. Of course there hadn't been a "hello" or "how are you" but simply straight to the point.

"I've been in town two days," Jack replied. "So, no."

"It's a nice farm, if you're into that sort of thing," his father stated. "Shouldn't be too difficult to find someone to take over."

"It needs a few updates before I list it."

Jack used the old key to let himself into the guesthouse. An instant aroma of thick, musty air smacked him in the face. Growing up, Jack had played out here on occasion, pretending he had his own fortress and was a knight or maybe even a cowboy in the old West. Sometimes his grandfather would let people down on their luck stay here. But now the one-room cottage sat empty and dark. Jack turned and reached for the curtain to let some much-needed light into the place.

"Are you still there?" his father asked.

Jack slid the drapes aside and coughed as a heavy cloud of dust wafted all around him. Last time he'd been in here, he and his grandfather had hung these curtains for the new minister of their church to stay until the parsonage was ready. Jack had used his first drill to put the screw into the wall for the rod. He'd forgotten all about that nugget of time until just now.

"I'm here," he replied.

"What are you doing? You sound odd."

Reliving the best memories of my life.

"Just taking a look through all the property."

Once the dust particles flitted through the stale air and settled, Jack allowed another good sweep of the place with his eyes. The old worn leather sofa sat against the wall across from the small fireplace. The mantel had no photos or decor. There were a few trinkets residing on the built-ins around the fireplace, but nothing of value. An old wooden rocker sat in the corner, and a small table with two chairs divided the open space between the living room and kitchen.

The place seemed the same…yet different. Depressing, really. The life that used to be here was now gone. A place that would be open to anyone who needed it, thanks to his grandfather's giving heart. But Jack couldn't get swept away in nostalgia. He couldn't afford to lose sight of his goal.

He knew he didn't want to sink a ton of money into this guesthouse, but he also wanted to make sure this piece of the property was another positive selling feature. He wanted to do right by his grandfather and make sure his legacy lived on. Jack wanted to make him proud while making the right renovations to sell to the right buyer.

Would that person plant rosebushes around the back entrance like his grandmother had before her health declined? Would the new owner fill the pastures with horses for their children and grandchildren to enjoy? Would there be sweet tea on the front porch swings while watching the sunsets?

"Is this a bad time?"

His father's exasperated tone pulled Jack from the memories once again.

"Was there something you wanted to discuss or were you just checking on the sale?" Jack asked.

Perhaps one day his father would ask how he was doing or if there was anything he could do to help. But Jack didn't believe today was going to be that day. The almighty dollar seemed to always be Logan Hart's only concern.

And if Jack wanted that promotion he'd worked so hard for, he'd have to make that his concern for the next couple of months.

"Just checking to see if you'd had any interest yet, that's all."

That's all. Of course it was. Jack shouldn't be surprised, or even hurt, yet he was both. Being back in Rosewood Valley, where his core childhood memories lived, Jack wished he could see his grandfather just one more time. To see that smile that left creases around his mouth and eyes, or to get solid life advice, or even just to sit around the kitchen table in silence... Just a few more minutes to make more memories would really help soothe his heart.

But the memories he had now were all he'd ever have. He wanted to honor that... He just didn't know how.

The adorable, persistent neighbor did, though. He hadn't heard her ideas, but she knew the area, and something told him she could be trusted.

"Why don't you text me with updates?" His father's tone had shifted to annoyed. "Clearly I'm interrupting some-

thing. I hope your head is on straight and you're not getting some wild idea about keeping the place."

Jack jerked and gripped his cell. "Why would I keep
it? I know nothing about farm life."

"No, you don't, so remember that."

His father disconnected the call without a goodbye.
Jack sighed as he slid his cell back into his pocket. He
couldn't let his father's sour mood get him down. Jack
had never known his dad to be any other way, but something about being in a place that had once brought so
much happiness and now created dread in his gut really
confused him.

Maybe he hadn't dealt with his mourning yet, or maybe
he was a jumble of nerves over this impending sale and
trying to get a promotion. Perhaps all of that rolled into
one weighty ball of anxiety... He truly didn't know but
had to stay focused. He couldn't let his memories, or his
father, divert him.

Thankfully his dad hadn't asked about the feed store.
Jack wasn't sure what to think about that place, and until
Rachel could find something to help him or the manager
came back and they could talk, Jack would have to keep
moving forward and focus on the farm. At least he could
control that portion of his life. He hoped.

"Can my dress be purple?"

Rachel eased herself down into one of the salon chairs
in her sister's shop. Jenn had recently come back home
after three years away and now she was engaged and going
to be a step-mommy to the sweetest little seven-year-old.
Paisley loved all things purple and was very invested in
the wedding planning.

"Purple?" Jenn gasped. "Is there any other color?"

"Well, you're wearing white," Paisley countered. "So I didn't know if I had to wear white, too."

Jenn finished braiding Paisley's hair and spun her toward the mirror to see the final result. "You can pick out any purple dress you want. This is not just my day, but yours, too. It needs to be special."

Rachel crossed her legs and watched the darling exchange between Jenn and Paisley. Paisley's parents had lost their lives in a car accident about a year ago and her uncle Luke had come to town as her guardian. He and Jenn had fallen in love, and the trio just seemed to click right into place—right along with Cookie, their stray pup. Their nontraditional family seemed like something from a heartwarming movie, and Rachel couldn't be happier for her sister, who had suffered her own loss when her husband had passed of a heart attack four years ago. All those broken hearts had somehow healed each other.

Rachel couldn't help how she felt, though. She could be thrilled for this union and still have her own hurt of waiting for the right one to come along. All she'd ever wanted was her own family, her own farm. She knew God would lead her in the right direction—she just sincerely hoped that she wasn't missing any signs or signals. Her ex-fiancé had really opened her eyes to what she wanted out of life and out of a man. She needed someone who shared her goals and interests. While love was important, there was so much more that went into a relationship, and she would be quite certain she'd found "the one" before she opened her heart again.

"So what color should I wear?" Rachel chimed in. "I know I won't look near as beautiful as the bride or the junior bridesmaid."

Jenn straightened and propped her hands on her hips.

"Honestly, I was thinking of having you, Violet and Erin all in either a sage green or a cream tone. I know that sounds like an odd combo with my dress being white, but I've seen some gorgeous weddings with that earthy color scheme and they were lovely."

"Jenn, you don't have to justify anything to me or anyone else. If that's what you like and you're happy, that's all that matters." Rachel blew out a sigh and caught her reflection in one of the many mirrors. "Now, what will we do with this hair of mine? I only do a braid. I wouldn't know how to do anything else."

Paisley hopped down from the salon chair and crossed to Rachel. She pursed her lips as she seemed to be studying and thinking of a new style. Rachel caught Jenn's amused gaze over Paisley's shoulder.

"What do we think, P?" Jenn asked. "Should we just let her keep the braid or give her something bold and new for the wedding?"

Bold and new. That was what Rachel wanted to be. Well, she had the bold down, according to her family and friends, but new? She'd been the same old Rachel for years. No new clothes, because she wasn't much of a shopper. No new hair, because she didn't need anything fancy for the farm. The only thing new in her life was the upcoming degree she'd been secretly working on.

"Since we're having an outdoor wedding, what if we curl her hair all down and maybe put some pretty flowers on one side?" Jenn suggested.

Rachel slid her attention back to Paisley. "You think that would work? I've never done my hair like that before."

Paisley's eyes widened and her toothless grin spread across her face. "You'd look like a garden fairy. That's so cool."

"Then maybe you need flowers in your hair, too." Rachel tapped the end of her nose. "Purple to match your dress, if that's okay with the bride."

Jenn nodded. "Absolutely. I want everyone to have a special day and feel beautiful. This is all about a new chapter in life."

Rachel eased back in her chair and pulled in a deep breath. "Well, now that my hair has been decided, what should we do for bridesmaids' dresses?"

"Go shopping," Jenn suggested. "I was actually going to see if all of my sisters were free this weekend to go on the hunt."

"And me?" Paisley asked as she bounced on her tiptoes.

"Of course my favorite bridesmaid will be there," Jenn assured her.

The clicking of paws on the hardwood had Rachel turning to see Cookie, the most adorable rescue spaniel-mix, slowly making her way into the salon.

Rachel turned her attention toward her sister. "I didn't think she was allowed in here."

"She's not when we're open," Jenn explained. "But when I'm closed, I let her roam free from the apartment."

Jenn lived in the loft upstairs. When she'd got into town, she decided to rent this salon and living space from Luke. Fast-forward several months and now the two were engaged and building a modest home on Four Sisters Ranch. They were going to make the most beautiful life together.

"So, back to shopping." Jenn took a seat in the salon chair Paisley had just vacated. "If we can all head out this weekend and make a fun girls' day, I think we could find the perfect dresses."

"I'm free," Rachel told her. "Are you going to have Mom come as well?"

"Of course. She needs to find something, too."

Paisley took a seat on the floor when Cookie rolled over onto her back for a belly rub. "Can we get lunch at that place that has those chocolate drinks?"

Rachel laughed as Jenn shook her head. "You and those drinks." Jenn sighed. "I'm not sure which dress place we'll go to, but I'll try to make sure we can get you a sweet treat while we're out. Deal?"

Paisley patted Cookie's belly and nodded, shaking her fresh curls. "Deal. I can't believe I have a whole family now. I always wanted aunts and uncles and grandparents. Now I have more than I ever thought."

She curled her little lips in as her chin quivered slightly. Rachel started to move, but Jenn was in motion, squatting down near Paisley.

"What is it?" Jenn asked.

Paisley glanced to Jenn with watery eyes. "I feel guilty for being happy. I love my mommy and daddy. Is that okay that I love you all, too?"

Rachel's heart broke for this sweet girl who'd lost so much at such a tender age. But God had a plan for all of them and had embraced Paisley with His arms and ushered her into this new life full of love and memories waiting to be made.

Jenn wrapped Paisley in her arms. "There is nothing to feel guilty about. I didn't know your parents, but I assure you that they would want you to be happy and loved. They would be so proud of the amazing, strong young lady you have become. So never feel guilty for living a good life."

As Rachel watched this exchange, she couldn't help but be proud of her sister for moving on from her own tragedy and living a good life for herself. She'd stumbled along the journey but had come home to where she belonged. She'd made her own way.

Now Rachel had to figure out how to make hers.

Chapter Four

Jack stared at the main-floor bathroom and wondered if the new buyer would love this bird wallpaper as a statement piece or find the yellow feathery friends revolting. Thankfully his doorbell rang and pulled him from the small space, because he'd also been considering tearing down the walls to make the room bigger and that would solve the wallpaper dilemma.

The bell chimed again through the main floor as he made his way down the hall toward the foyer. The glow from the porch lights illuminated a familiar face, and once again he couldn't ignore that little tug of attraction. He certainly didn't have time to consider dating…and definitely not with someone who wasn't even in his hometown. Long-distance relationships, especially with his busy life, would never work. Not to mention he'd spent years vying for his father's approval and working to get ahead. Jack just didn't have the mental space to feed into another relationship. He'd have to push aside any interest he had in the oldest Spencer sister.

Jack flicked the lock to open and eased the door wide. "Evening," he greeted her.

"Hey."

Her wide smile did nothing to help him ignore that

beauty of hers. This would be a difficult inner battle, no doubt.

"Is this a bad time?" she asked. "I probably should've texted first."

"No, this is fine." He stepped aside and gestured her in. "What's up?"

"I just wanted to fill you in on the store today and see about what you were thinking as far as renovations here."

She took a step inside and Jack closed the door as he watched her study the foyer. The area wasn't big by any means. The old farmhouse had been built decades ago with cutoff rooms. No modern open concept here. Just a small entryway table with an accent lamp, an area rug, and the dark-stained staircase and railing leading to the second-story bedrooms. One delicate glass globe nestled against the ceiling to supply minimal light. Nothing fancy, nothing exciting. And this would be the first impression when potential buyers came.

"We have to start in here," he commented before he could stop himself. "This is a very dull, boring space."

Rachel turned back to him with the sweetest smile, making those green eyes sparkle. "I think it's absolutely perfect. I might just add a nice bouquet of flowers on the table, but that's it. The staircase is grand and rich in color, the shades of blue in this rug really pop, and the adorable little light, it's all exactly what I'd put in my own home. A touch of charm and nostalgia."

He'd never looked at the house this way before, but just seeing the small space through her eyes had him wondering what she thought of the rest of the house. How would other buyers, other *locals*, view the place?

The only way to find out what would actually sell well in this small town would be to pick the mind of a resident.

Not to mention Rachel seemed quite convinced this place would be hers, so who better to get an idea than someone who already envisioned this as home?

"Should I start taking notes?" he asked, crossing his arms over his chest.

Rachel's dark arched brows drew in. "Notes?"

"Do you have time to go room by room and give me your first impressions of what you love and what you'd change?"

She shrugged one slender shoulder. "The fact that you want my honest opinion is almost laughable. If my family knew that, they'd tell you to run the other way."

"Outspoken, are you?" Jack asked.

Her lips quirked. "That's a matter of opinion."

"Well, I'll take that opinion so I can get this place ready to sell."

Her bright eyes dimmed, her shoulders fell just a touch, but enough that he noticed. He'd never let personal feelings enter into a business arrangement before and he couldn't start now. He had his own future to look out for. Besides, there were other farms. It wasn't like Rachel would be homeless. She just happened to have her sights set on this particular farm, and he needed someone who could buy at top dollar. If they could find a way to get her the funds, Jack would be all for this business deal. He'd worked with enough people who needed a little help. Maybe he could think of something, but he also couldn't compromise his own mission.

"I'm going to find a way to make this place mine," she assured him. "Being next to my family's land would mean everything to me. So I'm happy to tell you how to fix things I'd like changed."

Jack couldn't help but admire her determination. She didn't like taking no for an answer and had her eye on the proverbial prize. The more time he spent with her, the more he realized that while they were from two different worlds, they had a good bit in common.

"Let's start in here," he told her, gesturing toward the living room. "I know what I'd do differently, but let's hear what you think."

Jack remained in the wide arched doorway and watched as Rachel made her way into the room. She first went to the window seat and pointed.

"Do not remove this for any reason. This is the perfect spot to read on a rainy day or for a child to do homework or even have a quick nap."

"Duly noted." Though he wouldn't have taken that window seat out anyway. "What else?"

She turned toward the fireplace and smiled. "The wood detail on this mantel is so stunning. I can see Christmas stockings hanging here and a fire with a dog sleeping on the rug. I might swap out the old furniture, but that's not a must. The built-ins on either side of the mantel are a dream. I'd just have less clutter, but still homey and stylish."

As she spoke, he couldn't deny the love that came through her tone. She truly did have a passion for this old farmhouse, and that tug on his heart couldn't be ignored. His grandparents would want someone like Rachel to have this property. There had to be a way to find the right buyer for this place—someone who'd care for it—while still making the deal he needed to earn his promotion.

Jack hated that he had to work so hard for his father's approval. Each time he strove for perfection, he always thought that would be the last time and he'd ultimately win his father over. Maybe he'd even hear his dad say how proud he was.

But no. Jack still waited for that day, and he truly hoped this final thrust to the finish line would be the moment. He'd earn the respect and launch his own career and real estate office.

"Did I lose you when I mentioned the screened-in patio?"

Rachel's sweet tone pulled him from his thoughts. Jack needed to push his father to the back of his mind for the moment and concentrate on the remarkable woman before him. Yes, she might be helping him from her own desire for the property, but he needed to listen because someone like her was definitely buying the place.

Rachel's expressive gaze stared across the kitchen island as she waited for him to answer.

"Screened-in porch," he repeated, glancing out the patio doors that needed an update. "I think that's a great idea. An all-seasons patio would be a great addition, and any place someone can enjoy the beautiful views from inside would be a bonus."

A wide smile spread across her face, and Jack found himself returning the gesture. Something about her happiness and radiating light made some spark of joy burst inside him. He'd never met someone that seemed both driven and genuinely happy. Most people he knew were only happy if they were successful. Their careers drove them to find that happiness, but Rachel seemed to be the opposite. That drive inside her, even without having everything she wanted, was what made her so happy. She worked toward her goals but was content while doing so.

"Can you see a couple unwinding after a tough day on the farm?" Her voice took on a whimsical tone, and he knew she saw the scene playing out in her mind. "Maybe they've just put their kids to bed for the night and they're cuddled together on a nice cushy sofa. She's holding a hot cup of tea with honey and he's telling her of plans he's made for their future."

Jack found himself getting lost in this daydream of hers, and he could see the entire scenario, too. His mother had passed when he was just a toddler, so he hadn't seen a married couple sharing stolen moments or sharing dreams growing up. All he knew was work and reaching that next level on the proverbial career ladder. But Rachel had that picture-perfect upbringing, so she knew what she was talking about and it sounded like that was the life she wanted.

"Sounds like this isn't the first time you've thought of that moment." Jack leaned against the counter.

Rachel's eyes traveled from the window overlooking the backyard to him. That smile hadn't wavered, and the love in her eyes for this place, and for the life she so clearly wanted and deserved, said more than her words ever could. Why did she have to be so refreshing and give him a new glimpse into this land? Of all the times for an amazing woman to step into his life, now certainly did not line up with his goals or plans.

"Oh, I have," she assured him. "I mean, yes, I love this place, but in my mind, I've always seen a family and spending my days with the man I love and the life we were blessed with."

"You seem sure these blessings will happen."

Her brows drew in. "Why wouldn't I be? God has been so faithful to me through the years. Things might not happen in my time frame, but they happen in His, and I have to trust that won't change."

Jack's grandfather had always been strong in his faith, and during the summers Jack spent in Rosewood Valley, he recalled attending a little white church at the base of a hillside. The main thing he remembered were the dinners and the amazing food and how kind everyone seemed to be. Maybe that was why his grandparents always loved this town and the people here. Other than it being in the middle of nowhere, Jack couldn't recall a single negative thing about this community.

"What's causing that unusual smile on your face?" Rachel asked, tipping her head.

"Unusual smile?"

"Yeah. You normally scowl or look deep in thought."

Jack crossed his arms over his chest. "Is that so? I think I'm a pretty happy person."

"Really?" she volleyed back with a quirk of a brow. "So what were you just thinking of that had you happy?"

"Potato salad."

Rachel jerked back in surprise, then busted out laughing. "Well, I wasn't expecting that."

Jack shrugged. "You asked and that was it."

"I guess the saying is true that the way to a man's heart is through his stomach." She chuckled.

"Not necessarily," he countered. "I got to thinking of the church my grandfather attended and then I thought of all those amazing church picnics and that one lady who always made potato salad."

Rachel's mouth twitched as she seemed to stifle her laughter. "Oh, that was my mother."

"No way."

How had he forgotten that? Another memory from this town and these people that drew him deeper in.

She nodded with a sparkle in her eye. "I promise. She had us peeling potatoes the day before, so I definitely remember. She always took potato salad, fresh yeast rolls and some type of berry pie."

Jack shook his head in disbelief. "I hadn't thought about or had potato salad in years. I don't even recall the last time."

"Sounds like you need to come for dinner one night."

Jack cringed. Family dinner? That sounded way too involved. He hadn't come to town for anything of the sort.

"Well, that sure wiped the smile off your face," Rachel told him good-naturedly. "Now you're back to scowling. Is it dinner that upset you or the invitation?"

"I don't do family dinners."

"So eating alone is how you like to live?" Rachel turned and sighed as she moved toward the dining room. "That's sad. Maybe you should just try it and see if you like interacting with people on a personal level that has nothing to do with business or working."

Interesting that she'd zeroed in on his lifestyle. He didn't do much, if anything, that didn't involve work or making that next dollar. Rachel was not only beautiful and brilliant, but she was intuitive with other people's feelings, which said so much about her character.

Jack followed her through the doorway and into the formal dining area that hadn't been used since his grandmother passed of a stroke when Jack had been about six. The room had sat empty since. Jack could still see the table set with pristine white china when someone important came over—which had usually been their pastor and his family. But on occasion Jack's father would come for Thanksgiving or Christmas and those same dishes would be on display with beautiful floral centerpieces for the season. He didn't recall much from the short time he had with his grandmother, but he did remember her roses, how she liked to host and how she loved having her family all together.

"Hey. You okay?"

Rachel's caring tone pulled him from the past. Swallowing the lump in his throat, Jack nodded. The more time he spent in this town, in this *house*, the deeper he fell into all those past suppressed memories.

"Fine," he assured her, though he felt anything but.

He hadn't expected the rush of recollections going from room to room. He'd been in the house only a couple of days, but these clips of time rolling through his mind tugged at something on his heart he hadn't known existed. He couldn't be emotionally attached. That had been the first thing his father had taught him in business. Emotions didn't make the sales.

"You seem sad." Rachel took a step toward him and smoothed her braid over her shoulder. "If this is a bad time, I can go. Or we can discuss the feed store. I don't want you to be miserable."

"Miserable?" He hadn't been called that before. "I'm not, but I didn't expect to have this many attachments to a house. I mean, it's just walls."

Her mouth tipped to a soft smile. "But it's what happens inside those walls that touch our hearts and live in our minds forever."

An uncomfortable sense of unease coupled with a balm to his heart overcame him. He'd never had anyone discuss feelings like this before. And he'd never really had anyone touch his soul like this. He had no clue what to do with this mess of confusing thoughts.

"How do you do that?" he asked, thinking out loud. "Say things to make me feel like…"

Her brows drew in. "Like what?"

Jack shrugged, suddenly feeling rather silly. "Nothing. Let's talk about the feed store. Did you learn anything?"

Silence surrounded them, and he thought she'd press the topic, but after a moment she merely nodded and rested her hand on the high back of a cherry-stained dining chair.

"I did notice a pattern with the dates on the statements," she told him. "It looks to be every five days the deposits are significantly lower than the other days."

Business. Yes. This he could circle back to and make sense of.

"Five days," he murmured. "That's odd. What happens every five days?"

Rachel shook her head and sighed. "That I don't know, but the pattern started a few months ago."

"And nobody caught it until now?"

Unbelievable. Jack couldn't wait to talk to this manager, but for all he knew, that guy was the one stealing. Rachel might know the people of the town and be trusting, but he was skeptical. Having an outsider might be what was needed to find the answers. Nothing clouded Jack's judgment because he really didn't have an emotional tie here... except apparently to this old farmhouse.

"It's confusing for sure," she agreed. "And we'd never know how much is missing because we don't know what the deposits would've been. Of course we have the credit card transactions, but no clue as to the cash."

They could look at the dates of the sales and try to come up with a rough estimate of how much had been taken, but any amount was grounds for firing, as far as he was concerned. And maybe even getting the cops involved.

"That's really all I've found so far," Rachel added.

"That's important information. I just need to figure out the other missing pieces to this puzzle."

"In the morning I'm helping Dad ride the fence lines

and doing some repairs. So I can't be at the store. Ellen is working tomorrow, so I'm not too worried."

"I don't know Ellen, so I'm holding out my thoughts."

Rachel rolled her eyes as her delicate hand slipped from the chair. "Do you trust anyone?"

"I trust you."

That statement surprised him, but he realized it was true.

"That's it?" she asked.

She stared at him like she expected him to give her a whole list of names. But it was that bold green stare that had him stumbling over his thoughts. Everything about this woman intrigued him, from her larger-than-life personality to her subtle girl-next-door style. Not to mention her determination to help him find the thief from the feed store and her willingness to work with him on every bit of his inheritance.

"Don't you have a father?" she asked. "Surely you trust him."

Jack kicked that idea around for a moment before replying. "I suppose on some levels, yes. It's not like we discuss our deepest feelings or anything. But we work together, so I trust him there or I wouldn't be with the company."

She tilted her head. "That sounds more like a boss-employee relationship rather than father and son."

Jack started to say something, but Rachel waved a hand in the air, cutting him off. "Sorry. Not my business, so just ignore me. I'm sure you know by now that I open my mouth and speak before I think. I get myself into trouble sometimes."

"I'm aware, but you never have to apologize to me."

He took a step forward before he realized what he was doing, but when her head tipped up and her eyes widened, he stopped. Clearing his throat, he shoved his hands in his pockets. This woman managed to literally draw him in with just an innocent look and a concerned heart. He needed to watch his step or he could get into some real trouble here.

"I should probably go," she told him, as if sensing his unease. "I can definitely give you more ideas, especially for this main-floor bathroom, if you want."

Jack couldn't help but chuckle. "I doubt I could stop you from giving your opinion."

Her gaze flared, and she seemed to pause for a moment. "You should do that more often."

"What?" he asked.

"Laugh. Your whole face lights up and you don't look so miserable."

There was that word again. *Miserable.* He'd never thought himself to be a miserable person, but she seemed to have homed in on that for some reason.

"I'll make a mental note," he assured her.

Rachel made her way toward the other doorway across the dining room that led back into the foyer. He followed behind, not too close, but close enough to get some floral notes from her perfume or lotion.

"Thanks for coming by," he stated, reaching around to open the door for her. "I really do value this friendship we have."

Rachel tossed a glance over her shoulder and held him in place with that piercing stare. "Are we friends?"

Well, now he felt ridiculous if she was questioning him.

"I thought—"

"I'm teasing." She snickered. "So, since we're friends, I'll be sure to let Mama know you'll be coming for dinner soon. Good night, Jack."

She patted his cheek and headed out onto the wide porch, disappearing into the shadows of the night. Looked like he was going to a family dinner.

Chapter Five

"I suppose there's another fancy event here next weekend."

Rachel swung her leg over Sunshine and dismounted. "You mean a farm-to-table dinner? Yes, there is."

Her father still hadn't grasped the concept, but Rachel was so proud of Jenn for coming up with an idea to help bring more income to the farm. When it'd been on the brink of foreclosure just months ago, Rachel had been so worried. She'd even sold her house to help, moving into the apartment on her parents' property, but that hadn't been enough. Then Jenn had returned home with a great idea for an additional revenue stream.

Considering their mother made everything from scratch and they grew so much of their food and ingredients, why not tap into that by making delicious fixed-menu dinners for anyone who bought a ticket? They'd put a little work into the two-story barn behind the main house, and now the place was really starting to be a success with these dinners. They were even getting calls about booking private parties.

Jenn's fiancé had also purchased the front corner of the farm, which held a spacious barn where Luke could set up his large-animal vet office. He and Jenn were building a small cottage for them to begin their lives together with Paisley after the wedding.

Everything truly seemed to be falling into place for those she loved and cared for.

Rachel stepped up to the fence line and eased her heavy gloves on to check the barbed wire. She tugged on the knot around the post as her father checked the next post.

"Your mother was baking all night," he commented. "Today she said she was working on a new scalloped potato recipe. Sounds like a good dinner to me."

"Mom has never made a bad dinner."

"True."

Rachel moved down the line, loving this manual labor and the peaceful time with her father. She loved the sunshine on her face and making memories she'd have for a lifetime. This land meant everything to her, and she wanted nothing more than to obtain the property next door and grow their farm even more.

She couldn't help but feel a stronger bond to the place than just her love of the land. As George Hart had aged, she'd pop in to check on him. She'd bring food, claiming they had leftovers, just so he didn't have to worry about making his own. She'd worried about him taking care of such a large piece of property and all the livestock. He'd had workers that filtered in and out until he eventually sold off his animals, but Rachel felt like he needed a constant.

She'd formed a special relationship with George and absolutely adored that man. And maybe that was just another layer of reasoning as to why she felt so drawn to his grandson.

"I invited Jack to dinner," she added.

"Jack? George's grandson?" Her father let out a grunt,

whether of amusement or annoyance, she wasn't sure. "Heard he was back in town. I guess he's the one driving that fancy car."

Rachel bit the inside of her cheek. "With shoes to match."

"City boy, just like his dad. George's son never did appreciate what God gave him. Always wanted more. George was so happy when Jack would come for the summers, but then he grew up and went by way of his father and rarely came for visits. Crushed his heart."

"I would imagine so." Rachel stepped over a pile of manure and adjusted her hat to shield her face. "I get the impression Jack is a little mix of both his grandfather and his father. I can tell he cares about the land and the feed store, but he is planning on selling for a profit."

"Figured as much."

There went another grunt. Definitely disapproval. Will Spencer believed in hard work and sticking it out when times got tough. Which was just one of the reasons why they hadn't sold Four Sisters Ranch when financial hardships hit them. Will and Sarah Spencer were strong people, with faith that God would pull them through.

"Not everyone has a life of farming, Dad. Jack has made his life in San Francisco, and he'd like to get back to what he knows."

Her father turned his weathered, tired eyes toward her. "Just like I said. City boy. Wouldn't last a day putting in hard work on a farm. Best he sell the place before he makes the Circle H into something fancy like one of those short-term rentals or bed-and-breakfasts."

There was no secret her father was of the "no change" generation. He liked things the way they'd always been— nice and familiar.

"Sometimes change needs to take place in order for

growth and good things to happen," she offered. Like with their new event space, which he'd eventually come around to. "But I am working with him to get it ready to sell, so I won't let him go too fancy with it."

Her father straightened and adjusted his signature red suspenders. "Working with him, huh?" Yet another grunt. "And you invited him to dinner? Sounds like this is something serious."

Her heart did an extra flutter, which was absolutely ridiculous. Just because a handsome man came into town didn't mean anything. And just because he trusted her and needed her help with both of his properties didn't mean anything, either. She had her guard up. High walls had been erected around her heart after her failed engagement.

"Nothing serious," Rachel assured her dad. "We're just friends."

Friends. Just like she told him last night when she patted his smooth cheek. She should've never touched him because she hadn't realized the impact such an innocent gesture would have on her nerves.

She'd been on dates, she'd had serious boyfriends, but clearly the one long-term relationship she thought would end in a marriage had failed. No wonder a few encounters with her childhood crush and a minor touch had her completely flustered.

"I know my girls, and you have more interest in him than just as a friend."

Her father's concerned tone had her shifting from his studying gaze back to the fence.

"I promise, just friends. He's leaving as soon as the sales are final, and I'm trying to convince him to let me buy the farm on a lease or some arrangement that will benefit both of us."

"Honey, I know you've always wanted that farm," her father began with a sigh. "You've sacrificed so much helping us here and put your own dreams on hold. If I could get that place for you, I'd do it in a heartbeat. You deserve nothing less."

"I know you would." Rachel tugged on a wire and noted it had come loose. "I don't want you doing anything for me, Dad. You and Mom have given us the best life. I can make my own way."

As soon as she finished this online degree, she really felt she'd be on the right path. But the timing of that didn't coincide with the sale of the Circle H. She had to convince Jack to either let her work off some of the payments or convince him to let her lease. She didn't know his urgency to sell for top dollar; she didn't really see him as a money-hungry businessman. Something or someone else was driving him.

Maybe she could get him to open up, especially since he'd said he trusted her. If she understood where exactly he was coming from, perhaps she could find the perfect angle to get everything she wanted while he still made that sale.

"So when is Jack coming to dinner?" her father asked.

"Oh, we haven't set a day or anything. But he remembers Mom's potato salad from church dinners, so we're definitely going to have to have that."

Her father chuckled. "I haven't had her potato salad in quite some time. Sounds good to me. Maybe request ham, if you're picking."

Rachel smiled and finished her work on the broken wire. "I'll see what I can do."

As Rachel continued to work side by side with her father just like she had her entire life, she could only pray she'd be able to somehow obtain the adjoining farm so she could grow Four Sisters and have something substantial to last generations.

Jack stared at the email and blew out a frustrated sigh. He closed his laptop and set the device on the old end table next to the leather sofa and came to his feet. Waves of frustration rolled through him. Not only had Brian sold his intended property in record time and managed to set a company record of price per square foot, but he'd just landed another multimillion-dollar contract. For reasons Jack couldn't comprehend, his father seemed much too elated delivering that news.

Sometimes Jack wondered if his father loved the competition and the financial gain and success more than his only child. He truly believed his father loved him in his own way, but at times like this, he wished his dad would offer support or words of encouragement. Then again, maybe telling Jack how well Brian was doing was his father's strange way of motivating him.

It was times like this that Jack thought when and if he ever became a father, he sincerely hoped he put his son's needs and feelings as a top priority. Jack hoped to have a family of his own one day, but he would have to slow down enough to meet the right woman first. Still, the idea of passing his own legacy down seemed like a logical step… There were just many more steps to take before he could get to that point.

He picked up his glass of sweet tea and headed toward the kitchen. He'd been working on a different design layout for a couple of the rooms, but nothing was really sticking with him as the right way to go. He wanted each and every detail to be perfect. Not only for the potential buyer, but to pay homage to his grandparents. Yet his mind had been a jumbled mess since he arrived in town.

Why couldn't he focus? Real estate and design were all he knew, all he was good at. How could he even compete with Brian if he couldn't get his head on straight? He needed more of Rachel's thoughts. He needed her positivity and her outlook on life. She made him feel something he hadn't felt in a long, long time. He couldn't even pinpoint what that emotion was, but he knew the moment something impacted him in a negative manner, he wanted to turn to her.

What did that mean?

Maybe he could continue to spend time with her and get work done simultaneously. He'd still like to learn a little about the farm life and what type of buyer he was looking at, and he had no doubt Rachel would be the perfect person for that job. Not to mention he didn't know anyone else to ask.

After setting his tea back in the fridge, he pulled his cell from his pocket and fired off a text.

You home?

Like a teen with a silly crush, he stared at his phone as the three dots danced across the screen. Seconds later came the reply.

Yes

Jack shoved his phone back in his jacket and headed out the back door toward the garage. He slid into his car and maneuvered down the curvy tree-lined drive. The rolling farmland did have a certain appeal and a calming presence. He could see the draw to a laid-back lifestyle and to raising a family here and teaching core values. His father had grown up here but clearly didn't want any of that, though Jack had no doubt his grandfather hated to see his family go.

Jack's parents met in college in San Francisco and his father had never looked back. He couldn't help but wonder how different his life would've been if he'd grown up in Rosewood Valley. Would he have appreciated the farming more? Would he be married with his own little family? His priorities wouldn't be on the next sale or how stressed he was when his career didn't line up with his father's expectations.

He pulled into the neighboring drive and passed beneath the iron arch welcoming him to Four Sisters Ranch. He'd yet to see the other sisters, but he vaguely remembered them from his past visits. He wondered if they were all still close or if any had moved away and made a new life for themselves.

Rachel had mentioned she lived in the second barn behind the house, the one with a loft apartment. He really should've told her he was coming, but he'd made a rash decision. Something he figured she would appreciate and understand.

To the left seemed to be new construction for a cozy-looking cottage. He assumed that was Jenn and Luke's place, the couple Rachel had mentioned were getting married soon. A chapter like that in his life seemed so far away. He wasn't sure what type of husband or father he'd make. That wasn't exactly where his mind had been over the past several years.

Jack spotted the two-story white barn with chipped paint on the black-and-white doors leading into the horse stalls. He pulled around to the side looking for exterior steps and found them on the backside facing a pond. He hadn't been on this property in so long, he'd forgotten the beauty of the place. He could easily see why Rachel was so passionate about her work. The serenity of this place took his breath away. He could see the love and care, even if a few things needed some attention. Peeling paint didn't overshadow the large maple tree with the tire swing, or the colorful flowers vining down from the window boxes at the front of the main house. Swaying porch swings and mooing from the pastures made the farm come to life, and Jack understood why Rachel would want the land next door. Family and ranching meant everything to her. She wanted to grow what they'd started here, and he could appreciate her stance.

Which only made him feel guilty about the position he was in. Business couldn't get personal, ever. His father wouldn't have the most successful real estate firm in San Francisco if he'd let his feelings hinder each and every decision.

Jack stepped from his vehicle and started to lock it but realized this wasn't the city; he figured nobody would bother his things here on private property in the afternoon. He mounted the weathered stairs and tapped his knuckles on the sturdy door with a small window across the top.

The door seemed newer than the rest of the barn and he wondered if they'd made provisions for her to live above the horses' stalls.

The door flung open and Rachel's golden-brown hair went flying around her shoulders.

"Dad, I—"

She froze, her eyes widening as she took in her guest.

"Oh." She gripped the edge of the door. "Sorry. Dad

just called and I thought he was coming to tell me something else on his never-ending to-do list."

"No, just an unannounced visitor," he explained with a shrug. He should've clarified why he'd asked if she was home. "Is this a bad time?"

Rachel tucked her hair behind her ears and turned around to glance behind her, then back to him. "Um, no. This is fine."

"You sure?" he asked when she seemed hesitant. "It's not an emergency."

"This is absolutely fine." She took a step back and opened the door a bit more as she gestured him in. "I just got done helping Dad shoe a couple of our mares and then grabbed a quick shower. It was a rough morning. I probably look a mess since I thought I'd have a boring evening alone."

She didn't look a mess—quite the contrary. Her slightly damp hair fell down her back and she looked quite comfortable in her long-sleeve gray T-shirt and black sweatpants. Her bare feet got his attention...not that he took note of her pale pink–polished toes or anything.

"You look fine," he assured her, because telling her she was just as striking as any other time he'd seen her seemed a bit much.

Actually, he'd never seen her hair down. She always had that side braid falling over her shoulders. He hadn't expected all the waves, but then again, he hadn't given Rachel's hair much thought. Now he couldn't stop staring at how stunning she was. He hadn't anticipated another side to this farm girl or thought of how she'd be in her element at home. Just how many more versions of Rachel existed?

Jack crossed the threshold and glanced around the open loft area. The raw wood beams of the peaked ceiling were exposed, the small kitchen sat off to the left, a yellow sofa with a few throw pillows and coffee table were directly in front of him, and a perfectly made daybed with what appeared to be a handmade quilt sat tucked back in the corner. He assumed the two closed doors he noted were a closet and a restroom. The place was tiny but efficient, and of course tidy. He wouldn't expect anything less.

"Let me clean up my mess," she told him as she scurried back to the sofa area.

She grabbed a notebook and closed it, then stacked several papers on top and set them all on the raw-edge coffee table. She reached for her laptop, but not before he saw the screen.

"Is that an economics class?" he asked. "Are you teaching it or taking it?"

She let out an unladylike snort. "Oh, I'm definitely not teaching it. At this point, I'm not sure my fumbling around could be called taking it, either."

Jack inched closer to get a better view of the coursework. "Do you need help? Not to brag, but I aced all my business classes."

"Of course you did," she murmured as she sank down on the sofa. "And that might be bragging, but I don't care. I do need help."

Jack laughed and circled the table to sit next to her. "Do you ever ask for help?"

"I'm not too proud to admit I'm in over my head with this class." She set the computer on his lap and crisscrossed her feet on the sofa as she shifted to face him. "We have an essay due tomorrow and for the life of me I'm not sure what this professor is asking for. I mean, I can write papers, but I'm getting confused."

Her frustration was something he hadn't seen before. The Rachel he'd seen so far was determined and fearless.

"Let's have a look." Jack scrolled down and read the assignment. "So, what are you studying? What's your degree going to be in?"

"Business with an emphasis in agriculture. I want to help farmers make the most of their land, and I want to be in a position to educate new ranchers on proper setups and how to establish a firm foundation. There's nothing like building a legacy and passing down something so important as land and livestock. That's something that will last for generations if done correctly."

Jack shifted his focus from the computer screen to Rachel. Legacy. That was something that his grandfather had stressed as well. He'd wanted his farm to stay in the family and had passed the property down to Jack. But that was where the legacy would end. Another family, another lineage, would take the reins from here. A layer of guilt settled within him. He wanted to make his grandfather proud, but he honestly didn't know how, other than to find the perfect buyer who would appreciate and take care of the Circle H. At the same time, he also had to find a buyer willing to offer the highest dollar. He planned to make a legacy of his own in real estate.

Rachel shifted on the sofa and pulled his attention back to the present problem.

"You're so knowledgeable," he told her as he glanced from her to the screen. "I can't imagine people wouldn't trust you without a degree."

"Maybe not." She shrugged. "But I want to be seen as a professional and my degree will only help me."

"What does your family think about this?"

Rachel's gaze darted away as she sighed. "They don't know I'm doing this."

Surprised she'd keep anything from them, Jack eased farther into the sofa and forgot all about the essay. He'd been under the impression they were all very close-knit.

"Why don't they know?" he asked. "Aren't you proud of what you're doing? I'm sure they would be encouraging."

She blinked those wide eyes and his heart clenched. How did she keep affecting him in such a way that had his heart somehow getting involved? This girl next door, literally, had worked her way into his personal life, and with his concern and curiosity, he seemed to have worked his way into hers.

"I never thought to be proud," she admitted. "I'm doing this to better myself while helping others. I know I have the knowledge to help people, but I need that extra business sense to make better decisions for them and for our own farm. We almost lost it, and I won't let that happen. Ever."

There was that drive and determination once again. Not only did she have that strong will, but she also possessed an independence he hadn't seen in the women he'd dated.

Wait. He couldn't go down this road. He shouldn't be thinking about dating at all around her. His life wasn't here, and her life wasn't anywhere else. Besides, what did he know about relationships other than in the business sense? Other than his grandparents, he didn't really know people who stayed committed to each other in the name of love. Did people even marry for love anymore?

"So you're trying to earn a bigger income to provide for your family?" he asked.

"Partly so we have some security, but I think we'll be

fine now. Luke helped by purchasing some land for his new large-animal vet clinic, and when I sold my house last year—"

"You sold your house to save the farm?"

Rachel jerked at his abrupt question. "I sold my place to help, that's why I live up here now, but even with that, my parents still struggled."

She'd sold her house to live in a barn…all to save her family's legacy. The love she had for her family and this land continued to impress and surprise him. This type of commitment and concern went well beyond anything he'd ever experienced with his father. Jack wondered if she'd had much interaction with his grandfather. He had no doubt the two of them would've really hit it off and discussed all things farming.

"You seem speechless for the first time," she stated with a soft laugh. "I didn't mean to just let all of that out. Not many people know why I sold my house, and now you're the only one who knows about my online classes."

He truly felt humbled and touched that she'd opened herself up in such a vulnerable way. "Thank you for trusting me with all of that."

While she might be tough when it came to her goals, something he could appreciate, she had that soft interior that made her relatable. Actually, he could relate to her on all levels…which was starting to concern him.

"You already know I open my mouth and speak before thinking." She cringed, scrunching up her cute little nose. "It's a flaw."

"I don't see one flaw in you," he replied. "You're honest, which is refreshing, and you love deeply. Never apologize for being who you are."

That tender smile of hers spread even wider, and Jack

had a sinking feeling that if he stayed in town for too long, he'd lose himself in this amazing woman. Why was she still single? Did she date or did she throw herself into her work and now schooling?

Yes. The schooling. What he needed to shift his focus back to.

He adjusted the computer on his lap and scanned the assignment once again.

"Okay. Let's do this," he told her.

"Wait—you didn't come here to help me with a term paper. I'm sure there was something on your mind."

Rachel started to reach for the laptop, but he held it out of her reach.

"No, I didn't come for this," he agreed. "I came over because I was having an off day and you're the only person lately who makes me smile."

Her lips shaped into an O. Apparently his honesty shocked her, but he wasn't going to play games or pretend she didn't intrigue him. Even in their short time together, her genuine heart had opened wide and shown him just how he deserved to be treated.

Maybe if they'd reconnected like this under different circumstances, he'd attempt to see if they could start something beyond a friendship. But he had too much going on, and she was the settling-down type. Their life goals couldn't be more opposite.

"I don't think anyone has ever given me such a compliment before," she admitted after a yawning pause.

"I find that hard to believe," he countered. "Surely you've had boyfriends."

Rachel nodded. "And a fiancé."

Surprised, Jack set the computer on the coffee table

and adjusted so he could face her better. He stared into her striking green eyes.

"You were going to marry a man who never told you that you make him smile?" Jack asked.

Her brows drew together. "I never really thought about it. I mean, he would tell me he loved me and that I was pretty, but we weren't meant to be."

"What happened?" he asked, then immediately shook his head. "Sorry. That's just me being nosy. You don't have to answer."

"It's fine." She offered him another one of her sweet smiles as she smoothed her hair over one shoulder. "Of course I was heartbroken at first when we split, but I can look back and see that God had another plan for me. I don't know exactly what that looks like, but He was protecting me from a marriage that would've failed. Tyler and I were too different. He didn't appreciate the farm life and this is my one true passion."

Jack couldn't imagine a man walking away from someone so vibrant and full of life. Had this Tyler guy not even tried to compromise to keep Rachel? From what he could tell, she had simple needs. She valued her family and the farm. She didn't need flashy expensive things to make her happy. Perhaps that was why he found her so refreshing, as she breathed a new aspect of life into him. In fact, spending time with her had made him more and more curious to reconnect with farm life, the way he had during those summers with his grandpa.

"How soon is your term paper due?" he asked, gesturing to the laptop.

"Friday. Why?"

Jack came to his feet and extended his hand. "Care to show this city boy a little more of this farm life?"

   A bright sparkle shimmered in her eyes, and he didn't think she could be more beautiful, but her entire face lit up at his suggestion. And the moment she slid her delicate hand in his, he knew he'd got in deeper than he'd ever intended.

Chapter Six

Sure, Rachel needed to work on her paper, but she'd felt some unexpected connection with Jack after telling him all her secrets—why had she gone into so much detail about her class and followed it up with her failed engagement? When he'd asked about her farm, there was no way she could turn him down.

"Ever ridden a horse?" she asked, leading him through the aisle between the stalls.

"A few times with my grandfather, but that was long ago."

She glanced down to his shoes and stopped. "You want me to find you something else to put on?"

Jack's eyes followed hers as he rocked back on his heels and chuckled. "My shoes have never been so offensive as they are to you. But I think I'll be fine."

"Suit yourself," she muttered as she turned to head into the tack room. "I've just never met someone who wears dress shoes for everything."

"And now you have," he joked.

She searched for the right saddles and blankets for the two horses she wanted to take out. Sunshine was hers, no question. She thought about putting Jack on Starlight but decided Champ would be a better fit.

"How many horses do you all have?" he asked.

Rachel passed him a saddle and he took it with a grunt. She smiled as she turned back for the other one.

"We have seven now. We used to have twelve but had to sell some for financial reasons."

Rachel set everything down in the aisle before she opened Champ's stall. She slid her hand down his velvety nose. The soft hair against her fingertips always calmed any nerves or fears. Animals were so trusting and loving; no matter the type of day you had, they were always a constant friend.

"You'll be riding Champ." She glanced over her shoulder to find Jack next to her. "He's four and gentle. Definitely good for a beginner."

"Beginner?" he scoffed. "I bet I can remember everything without you telling me."

Rachel stepped aside and held her hands up. "By all means. Help yourself. Just watch you don't scratch those shiny shoes."

"Would it make you feel better if you got me some boots?" he asked.

"Oh, I don't want to take you out of your element," she joked as she moved to the next stall with Sunshine. "You do your thing and I'll do mine."

He muttered something beneath his breath while Rachel grabbed a blanket and moved into Sunshine's area. She smoothed her hand down the mare's back and gave her a good pat.

Jack's soft words to Champ warmed Rachel's heart. Any man who loved animals had a good soul. She'd learned quite a bit about her ex when he'd not really cared about her world or the care of the livestock. He assumed others would take care of everything, and horses and farms were glamorous. She'd had such tunnel vision while looking ahead to being a wife and mother, she hadn't considered he'd been the wrong man for her. It wasn't until she came to the realization he didn't have a servant's heart that her world had crumbled. God had given her signs all along, from his excuses to avoid family dinners, to his drive for working above spending a quiet Sunday afternoon with her. She hadn't wanted to see the negativity since she knew nobody was perfect.

Letting Tyler go had been the most difficult decision, yet the only one she could've made. The growth from that time in her life had prepared her, she hoped, for when God sent the right man her way. But he would have to be above and beyond for her to let those walls down ever again. At times she wondered if she was just climbing a mountain with no peak in sight.

Not that she *needed* a man to fulfill her, but she wanted someone to come home to. She wanted someone to share her days with and make a lifetime of memories. She hoped there was a man who was just waiting on her as well.

Jack groaned and muttered something beneath his breath, snapping her attention from her thoughts.

She glanced through the bars on the wall separating the stall.

"Problem?" she asked.

He glanced down and shook his head. "Oh, no. Just stepped in a pile because I wasn't paying attention."

Rachel couldn't suppress her laughter.

His dark eyes came up to meet hers and his own lips twitched in amusement. "Go ahead—laugh it up."

"Hope you don't lose the shine on those." She chuckled.

"I have shoe polish."

Rachel rolled her eyes. "Of course you do."

"Are you even going to comment on how well I saddled Champ?"

She shifted her gaze to the blanket and saddle and nodded. "Well done. You do remember a few of the things you learned from your grandfather."

"I didn't think I would, but I could hear his voice in my head guiding me through."

Rachel's amusement slipped as nostalgia slid into place. "That must be special to still know the sound of his voice."

Jack's hand smoothed down the chocolate mane on Champ's neck. "That's something else I thought I wouldn't remember. It's nice to know I still have that memory. I guess coming back has tapped into those core childhood moments."

"Are you comforted by that or do they make you sad?"

He paused as if trying to gather his thoughts. Sunshine neighed and bobbed her nose, more than ready to get out into the wide-open fields.

"I'm a little of both, I think," he admitted.

"I guess that's just the emotions that come with losing someone you love dearly."

Rachel led Sunshine from the stall and held the reins in her hand. "You ready to go or do you want that pair of boots now?"

He mimicked her as he and Champ came out into the aisle. "At this point these shoes might be done for. No need to change them. I've never worn cowboy boots anyway. I wouldn't even know how to walk in them."

"One foot in front of the other," she joked.

"But if I started that cowboy swagger, I wouldn't be able to keep the women away, and I don't have time for a relationship right now."

He winked and her heart fluttered again. He didn't

need the boots or the swagger to make her want to get to know him better. She'd gone well beyond that point, but he'd made it clear he didn't have time for anything, and hadn't she learned her lesson once already? Workaholics didn't make time for the necessities in life, and her core values all hinged around God, family and her farm. Everything else was just an added bonus.

Her ex hadn't made her family a priority in his life. In Rachel's eyes, they were a package deal and anyone would be lucky to have her sisters and her parents in their lives. Not only would the next person she considered letting into her life need to be in tune with her love of the farm, but he would also have to love her family as much as she did.

"I'll be sure to keep the ladies away from you," she assured him with a laugh. "But it's not like Rosewood Valley is crawling with bachelorettes. I mean, there's my two sisters, Erin and Violet, then me and a few others, but most women get married pretty young here, and we have a very low divorce rate."

Rachel headed toward the wide opening at the other end of the barn and Jack followed behind her. She didn't recall a time when her ex asked about her farm or anything to do with the livestock. Jack had a caring heart or he wouldn't have asked. Maybe because he wanted to sell and wanted to know more about the lifestyle, but she was going to pour her soul into showing him why Rosewood Valley was heaven on earth anyway.

"This town is like something from an old movie," he stated once they stepped into the field. "Or stuck in time perhaps. Perfect marriages, picturesque town, family traditions."

Rachel stopped and pulled her hair over her shoulder to start her braid. No way could she ride with her hair flying in the wind. With expert fingers, she wound her strands together and pulled the band from her wrist to secure everything.

"First of all," she stated after her hair was in place, "no marriage is perfect. There are imperfect people who find someone who complements their flaws. And, yes, our town is amazing and our values really make us stand out. We like our little pocket of the world."

"I can admit Rosewood Valley is an amazing place." He glanced around the open area toward the hills in the distance and shielded his eyes from the afternoon sun. "I definitely don't see this much sky back home."

Rachel gripped her reins as she placed one hand on her pommel and slid her foot into the stirrup. She slung one leg over the saddle and settled into her favorite worn spot. As far as she was concerned, this was the best seat and view in the world. Rachel glanced down and offered Jack a smile.

"We're growing on you," she informed him. "You're never going to want to leave."

He put his foot into his own stirrup and did a bounce to get up into the saddle. He took a couple of tries, but ultimately got it right. The fact he was trying, that he was open to this part of her life, shouldn't have her so happy. He wasn't staying and he wasn't some date. But still, it was nice to get out and not be working or doing school stuff. She could relax and just enjoy what she'd been blessed with.

"Nice job," she praised. "You aren't as rusty as you thought."

"Oh, I'm sure I'll feel this in the morning."

Rachel nodded in agreement. "No doubt, but for now, let's enjoy this gorgeous evening. There's nothing like a sunset on the farm. Plus, fall and winter will be here before we know it, so I want to soak up all of this beautiful weather."

"Does it get cold here?"

"Pretty cold." She tapped her heel on Sunshine's flank to get her moving. "We have all seasons, but that's just another reason I love it here. I wouldn't want to live somewhere it's cold or hot all the time. I like the difference the mountains have to offer."

Jack and Champ fell into a cadence beside her, and Rachel lifted her face to the sun.

"I couldn't imagine living anywhere else," she added as she pulled in a deep breath of fresh air.

For a moment, the peaceful silence enveloped them. Rachel wondered where his thoughts had headed and if the town was indeed getting to him. She couldn't imagine anyone stepping foot here and not falling in love. Who wanted to live with stress and high-rises and crowds?

"Tell me about your sisters."

Jack's statement broke the silence, and a warmth instantly spread through her. He wanted to know her better. But he could also just be filling the quiet space. Rachel really didn't think so. She hadn't known Jack long, but she knew George, and Rachel saw so many similarities between the two. Kind and considerate, to name just a couple.

"Well, I've told you Jenn came back to town after being gone for three years. Her first husband passed, and she ran from the pain. Now that she's back, she has Luke and his niece whom he has guardianship of. Her name is Paisley. And as you know, Jenn and Luke are getting married next month. That's the very short version of her story."

"Good for her," Jack replied.

Rachel smiled and gestured toward another open pasture. "Head that way. And, yes, I'm thrilled they all three found each other. Then there's Violet. She's a small-animal vet in town and single. My other sister Erin is an elementary teacher. She's also single, but she was engaged once, and then he left town as a missionary and he's been gone for years. My sisters and I don't know that she ever got over him, but we don't bring up that sore subject."

Jack made a soft hum beneath his breath as if taking all that in. He genuinely seemed interested in what she was saying, so she went on.

"We've always been close," Rachel added. "Other than the few years Jenn was gone, but now that she's back, our family is stronger than ever. And we've started a farm-to-table event business that has really taken off, so that's something we all work on together as well."

"Are you all always together?" he asked.

"Not all of the time. We definitely have our own interests and hobbies."

Jack glanced her way. "What are some of yours?"

"I love the farm and the livestock and—"

"Outside of farm life," he corrected.

Rachel pursed her lips as they headed toward one of the ponds on the property. Outside of the farm…did she have hobbies?

"I like to eat. Does that count?" She laughed.

Jack's soft chuckle had her heart clenching once again. How did he make all these dormant feelings rise to the surface?

"We'll start there," he replied. "You have a favorite food?"

"Anything I don't have to make." Their horses came to a stop at the edge of the pond and Rachel shifted to face him. "I'm not a bad cook, but cooking for one is depressing. I guess that's why I love this new event business my family started. Cooking for a crowd is fun, and I love to see people come together and fellowship in whatever way brings them joy."

"You can cook for me anytime," he informed her. "I'm sick of eating grilled cheese sandwiches."

Rachel quirked a brow. "You're still coming to family dinner sometime, but I'll make you something. What's your favorite meal?"

He shook his head. "Let's not do the family dinner. Remember? I don't do those. But I wouldn't turn down a meal from your kitchen. Do you have a specialty?"

"I can make some pretty good chicken and dumplings." Rachel swung her leg over the saddle and hopped down. She led Sunshine to a small nearby tree and secured the reins. "Go ahead and have a seat with me. We'll take a rest from riding so maybe you won't be too sore tomorrow."

Without a word, Jack dismounted, led his horse near hers and tied his own knot. Certainly not like she had, but Champ and Sunshine wouldn't go anywhere regardless. Rachel always tied her horse to be safe.

When Jack eased down on the grass beside her, Rachel stretched her legs out and leaned back on her hands. She closed her eyes and pulled in a deep breath.

"Do you hear that?" she murmured.

"Hear what?"

"Exactly. Just the peaceful evening." She kept her eyes closed, trying to lock this moment inside. "We aren't worried about the missing funds or how I'm going to get the Circle H. Sometimes I just need to ride out here to pray and clear my head."

"And do you do that often?"

Jack's question had her turning her attention back to

him. His dark eyes held hers and she felt another jolt of attraction.

"Well, I pray all the time," she informed him. "Multiple times a day, but I don't get here as often as I'd like with all the work on the farm and schooling."

"And I've thrown the feed store into the mix," he added.

"I agreed to take that on," she said. "I wasn't forced. Besides, I'm hoping we can still work something out for the ranch. Maybe a lease or rent or anything until I can gain my footing and buy it outright."

Jack started to open his mouth, but she held up a hand to stop him.

"I know—you have some reason to get this sold soon and for a lot of money and I'm not in a position to help you right now." She weighed her next words carefully. "I'm also not helping with the feed store and renovation ideas because I want you to do me a favor. I'm doing all of this because I loved your grandfather. But I am confident we can come to some type of agreement that will benefit both of us regarding your inheritance. I just… I can't be this close to something I've always dreamed of and watch it slip through my hands."

Jack didn't say a word. He simply stared back at her with a look in his eyes she couldn't quite label. Maybe guilt with a little bit of worry. She wished he'd just tell her the bind he was in so she could see if there was any chance she could help.

But when he remained silent, Rachel directed her gaze back to the pond and the glistening sun on the water and started that praying she always came here for.

Chapter Seven

"You don't think the entire wall should be one large open shower?"

Jack waited for Rachel's reply, but she leaned against the door frame with her arms crossed and her brows drawn as if trying to imagine the space.

"Sounds very modern," she finally stated. "I mean, I haven't seen anything like that, but maybe in the main bedroom it wouldn't be a terrible idea. But there has to be a big soaker tub. I mean, if you're going to go all out in here, you might as well. Farmers are worn out and sometimes just need a nice hot bath at the end of the day."

Jack already had that on his mind as well, but he welcomed all input that would be great selling points.

"What are your thoughts on a set of patio doors leading out back off this main suite?" he asked.

Rachel turned to look at the bedroom in question and he followed her back into the small space. Boxes sat atop the bed from things he'd been storing up to give away. Books and old collectibles that didn't have any sentimental value were ready to be donated.

"I think it would make this room look larger," she agreed, then pointed toward a narrow window. "I assume you'd put it there?"

Jack nodded. "Between the doors letting more light in and a brighter paint color, it would help make the space look larger."

"A pale yellow or pale blue," she murmured. "We could paint this furniture to save money."

"Buying will be quicker and easier."

Rachel snorted as she turned back to face him. "What if I paint the furniture while you focus on other things?"

"I think you're busy enough, and I'm positive you didn't think that through before you offered." He chuckled.

Her little nose scrunched, and he decided it might be the most adorable gesture he'd ever seen.

"You already know me well," she stated. "I just hate buying something when I know I can do it myself. But you're right. Between the store and the farm, plus my schooling…"

"And you might want to have a social life."

She crossed her arms over her chest. "Do you have a social life?"

He spread his hands out wide. "This is it. You and me. That's all the social life I've had since coming to town."

"And what about back home?" she asked. "Do you get out and do something not work related?"

"I take potential clients to dinner."

Her arms dropped to her sides as she shook her head. "I rest my case. All work. My ex-fiancé never took time for anything he loved to do, either."

Her ex. She'd touched on him before, and Jack didn't care for the faceless man. How could anyone not adore Rachel and this daydream life she wanted? Granted, this wasn't a life for him, but for someone who lived here and knew the town and the people, he couldn't imagine letting Rachel slip from his life if he was engaged to her.

But he wasn't engaged and he wasn't getting tangled in a relationship or farming.

They needed to discuss the main bath, so Jack started toward the door to the hallway and Rachel followed.

"How recent was the engagement?" he asked casually as he crossed the landing to go downstairs to the first floor.

"A couple years ago. He hated farm life and always wanted me to move away. I kept hoping and praying he'd see the beauty here and want to be part of the world I envisioned."

The sad tone that slid through her words made Jack wonder if she missed the man or just the life she'd dreamed of. A short burst of jealousy hit him, and he had no idea why. Jack had no ties to Rachel and he certainly didn't know the man in her past. So why did he instantly have this need to compare himself to a stranger?

"You want to raise your family here and carry on traditions and grow your property." Jack stopped in the foyer before heading down the hall toward the main-floor bath. "You love livestock and being there for your family. I can't imagine you ever leaving, and anyone who tried to get you to is foolish."

Rachel stopped on the bottom step and rested her hand on the wooden banister. Those green eyes fixed right on him, and he couldn't move if he wanted to. How could someone be so down-to-earth, yet so amazing and brilliant and captivating at the same time? There were so many layers to her, yet he thought he had her figured out...and he was fascinated and attracted to everything he saw.

He was no different from her ex, though. He knew nothing of how to feed a relationship, and he certainly hadn't a clue about farming.

"You've only known me a short time and already know my heart," she murmured.

His chest tightened as he moved toward her, closing a bit of the gap between them. That one step beneath her put them at eye level…as if he needed another reason to find himself utterly entranced by her. Those emerald eyes had a darker ring around them that he shouldn't care about, but suddenly he cared about every single thing when it came to Rachel.

No, not suddenly. Since she'd ridden up on that horse and professed her childhood crush. There was no denying that pull, yet frustration gripped him because he couldn't explain it. He'd always had control over his emotions—over everything in his life, really.

Or so he'd thought. Then Rachel swept into his neat and tidy world and completely disassembled every thought he'd had.

"Why are you looking at me that way?"

Her whispered words snapped him back to the moment and the fact that he was standing extremely close to her now.

"I'm just amazed that anyone who professed to love you and spend his life with you could simply walk away."

Her gaze traveled over his face. "I'm not sure how simple it was, but the parting was definitely for the best. I guess I walked away, too. At least, mentally."

Jack found himself resting his hand on top of hers, giving a reassuring squeeze. "Loss is still difficult," he explained. His heart squeezed for the hurt she must've felt at her broken engagement.

"I have to look at that experience as a life lesson and learn from it." She offered another one of her signature sweet smiles. "That's the only way to overcome heart-ache of any kind."

"I'm figuring that out," he told her. "I didn't realize how much emotion I had after my grandfather's passing, but being in town and surrounded by his things has really made me think and reflect."

Rachel took that final step down and tipped her head to keep eye contact.

"George was an amazing man," she told him. "The town definitely misses his presence."

Jack eased his hand from hers, not wanting to make her uncomfortable. She dropped her hand to her side, and her warmth beneath his palm left a void. That simple, innocent touch had been a mistake, but he hadn't been able to stop himself. She hadn't jerked beneath his touch and she'd smiled, so apparently she hadn't been bothered.

And the way she stared right back at him, like she could see into his soul, seemed to pull that string binding them together even tighter. This couldn't happen, *shouldn't* happen. He'd be no different from the guy who walked away from her, and hadn't Jack just called him foolish? Keeping their relationship strictly working and friendly was the only way he could move on from his experiences in Rosewood Valley with a clear conscience.

"Speaking of my grandfather, anything else on the store?" Jack asked as he turned to head toward the main bath.

She paused a moment. "The manager is due back tomorrow, so I'm going to casually discuss how business is doing since George's passing, whether the numbers are up or down, and just see if I can get him talking."

Jack reached into the powder room and flicked on the

switch. "That's great. I'll be interested in what he has to say."

He stepped aside so Rachel could look into the small space without being crowded.

"What are you thinking in here?" he asked.

"Don't touch these amazing floors," she commanded, pointing to the black-and-white hexagon tiles. "Not only are they classic and timeless, but anything will go with them."

"Buyers like that touch of nostalgia and original charm," he added.

"Buyers might, but I'm the only buyer you need to impress."

That guilt gripped at him once again. For the first time in his business career, he was letting his heart get involved in his decision. And doing that would only leave him at a standstill and unable to advance to the ultimate real estate mogul he'd always striven to be. He didn't know how to be anything else other than a businessman and he was good at his job. He had no shame in wanting more success or to make his father proud.

"What do you think about a walk-in shower and making a glass wall so it looks more open and the space doesn't feel so small?"

Jack nodded. "I'm impressed. I like that idea."

"I might be country, but I have good taste."

"You definitely do. What else?"

She moved in and stared at the wall with the vanity. Her braid fell over her shoulder and he found himself following the lighter strands weaving in and out all the way down to the tip.

"What about making this an accent wall with a bold paper?" she asked, glancing back at him.

"I think that would be a nice touch. Is that something you want to pick out?"

The brightest smile spread across her face as her brows shot up. "Oh, I definitely do. I might not have time for the furniture painting, but I can online shop like a champ."

Jack chuckled. He had no doubt she'd put her all into this project, and if they were using his dime, all the better for her.

"Get me a few suggestions in the next week or so. I've got a contractor coming in the morning, and I'd really like to push through and have this for sale in the next month."

Rachel turned to face him fully and crossed her arms over her chest. "I really want to discuss a lease with the option to buy. I know you are hard-pressed to sell, but I can't come up with a solution if I don't really know what's going on."

He didn't think she'd ever come up with a solution to appease both of them unless she had a good chunk of money, and from her own account, she did not.

"Are you strapped for cash?" she asked. "Because I'm sure we can figure something out. George would want someone to have this property who would take care of it and make it thrive."

Yes, he knew all of that but needed to address the most important thing.

"I'm not strapped for cash," he assured her. "I'm trying to get a promotion with my firm. No, I'm not trying. I'm *going* to get that promotion."

"And how many people are vying for this position?" she asked.

"Just one other."

Rachel pursed her lips and ultimately nodded. "You'll

get the job and I'll be able to get the house. We just have to put our heads together on this."

She didn't know his father very well. The man didn't bend or break for anyone…not even his own son. Jack wasn't about to get into the dealings with his dad right now. Rachel seemed too sweet a person to associate with Logan Hart.

"It's getting late," she stated with a sigh. "I should probably get going and work on that paper of mine. It's not going to write itself."

"When you're done, email it to me and I'll double-check everything to make sure you ace it."

Rachel jerked as her arms fell to her sides. "You don't have to do that. I mean, I would take your help, but you're just as busy as I am."

Jack shrugged. "I'm not working on anything tonight. I'll text you my email. You're doing the grunt work. I'm just going to make sure it's polished."

Rachel's gentle laugh echoed in the small bathroom. "You really are a great guy. I don't know anyone else who would offer to spend free time working on an econ assignment that wasn't even his. But I'm a little overwhelmed with the topic and afraid I'll sound like I don't know what I'm talking about."

"All the more reason to let a friend help."

She took a step forward and patted his cheek. "Perfect, friend. I'll send that over later and you can come to my place for dinner tomorrow. Deal?"

"I won't turn that down and I'm definitely getting the better end of the deal," he joked.

She eased by him and moved into the hallway. "You won't say that once you dig into the globalization on emerging economies."

He cringed. "Ouch."

"Exactly."

Jack followed her to the foyer and reached around to get the door for her. His arm briefly brushed against hers and she gave a slight jolt, then a soft smile.

"Good night, Jack. See you tomorrow about seven."

Jack watched as she went out and untied her horse from the post near the porch. His grandfather would never want that hitching post removed, and Jack had no intention of taking anything away from this farm that made it special and operational. Rachel would rather travel by horse than car anyway, and since she lived at the neighboring farm, her horse just made sense.

He couldn't wipe the smile off his face as he closed the door once she'd ridden away. He kept thinking he'd never met anyone quite like her, and the more he was around her, the more he figured he'd never meet anyone this extraordinary again.

So now where did that leave him other than torn between his family and his heart?

Chapter Eight

Rabbit and swine feed orders were placed, and Rachel felt quite accomplished with her first order. With Walt still out, she didn't want the shelves to start looking bare and she knew enough about feed to know what was sold here. Granted, she'd never placed an order before, but after a couple of hours spent searching through invoices and then getting on the phone to customer service of a supplier, the deed was done.

Rachel leaned back in the old creaky office chair and blew out a sigh. Her first real task down since starting her part-time employment here. She wasn't going to go overboard with restocking, but the feed in a feed store was a rather important part.

"Busy?"

Rachel glanced from the computer screen displaying her email confirmation to the open doorway where Jack stood with a smile.

Rachel returned his pleasant gesture with one of her own. "Just restocking a couple things. Did you come to check up on me?"

He shrugged as he stepped into the office. The dark jeans and long-sleeve black button-up shirt still seemed dressy and a little fancy, but she didn't mind. She was growing rather fond of his upper-class style.

"I thought I'd hang here today while I'm waiting to hear from a couple contractors," he explained. "Maybe you can show me a bit more about this place since I do own the store."

Interesting that he wanted to discover more. She wasn't sure of his intent on this part of his inheritance, but the fact that he wanted to soak up more information warmed her heart. This was definitely an area she could teach. She'd been coming to the feed store with her dad since she was a kid and knew the floor like the back of her hand.

"Maybe we can put our heads together and figure out these off-putting numbers as well," he added.

"That would be great," she agreed. "I'd hate to have Walt come back to terrible news and no answers."

Rachel pushed the rolling chair back and came to her feet. "Well, let's get you started on a grand tour and Feed Store 101 lesson."

Jack stepped forward and glanced around the some-what messy desk. He grabbed a pen from the old mason jar and rifled around until he found a notebook. Rachel glanced at the items in his hand, then to him.

"I need to take notes," he explained.

Stunned, Rachel shook her head in amazement. "I've never met anyone like you," she murmured.

"Probably not," he agreed as he led her from the office.

Not only was he eager to learn more, but he wanted to absorb the information given. She truly hated when she compared Jack to Tyler. They were two completely different men with totally different roles in her life. But she was human and couldn't help herself. Lately, she couldn't help but wonder if they could be more if they weren't from completely different worlds and didn't have totally opposite goals.

Rachel stepped into the hallway behind Jack, but he stepped aside to let her through.

"Let's start with some basics that our customers come in for," she started as she headed toward the open sales area. "Feed is obviously the biggest seller. We supply farms from all over, not only this county, but surrounding counties as well. George really had a knack for customer loyalty, and he made solid relationships with the farmers. I'm sure he'd want generations to know they can rely on All Good Things."

"That's what I hope to accomplish," Jack replied. "I want my grandfather's legacy to live on whether I remain the owner or someone else takes over."

Yeah, Rachel really wanted to know this place was secure, too. And maybe selfishly she wanted him to keep this part of his inheritance for himself. She wasn't ready for him to leave town with no reason to return. Which only proved as a reminder that the last time she let her guard down, she'd got her heart broken. She was going into this with her eyes wide open and her heart behind a shield of protection.

"Let's start in the front and work our way to the back," she suggested.

Jack followed her down the aisle that led to the front display of seasonal items.

"This display right inside the door is always done with whatever is hot at the moment," she explained. "Obviously since summer is sadly coming to an end, mums and fodder are center stage."

"Summer is your favorite season?" he asked.

Rachel turned to focus on him and not the rust and yellow mums. "I love all the seasons, but I definitely love the warmth of summer. Too bad you won't be in town to see all the gorgeous foliage in about a month."

Why did she let that slip out? She didn't want to think about him leaving, let alone talk about it.

He opened his mouth to say something just as the chime on the front door echoed through the old two-story barn. Rachel turned to greet the customer. She assumed Myles was around here somewhere. She'd seen his car and heard someone puttering around in the back of the store.

But her mother breezed in with a smile and a plate of something from her kitchen. The woman never went anywhere without some gift or treat for whomever she was visiting.

"Mom. What are you doing here?"

Rachel crossed to her mom and gave her a hug.

"Well, you've been so busy lately, I feel like I never see you." She extended the covered plate. "I made some cranberry orange muffin tops. I know they're your favorite."

Rachel loved her mother's giving, thoughtful heart. Sarah Spencer never had a negative or unkind remark and was always finding ways to bring others joy. Rachel couldn't think of a better role model to look up to.

"I'm sorry I've been so swamped," Rachel told her mom. "I promise to come by the house this weekend. Dad and I have been a little busy on the farm and then with trying to help out here while Walt is gone, and I'm showing Jack a few things."

Not to mention her schooling, which she hoped to surprise her family with once she was all done and a success.

"Yes, that's another reason I stopped by." Her mother's bright gaze darted over Rachel's shoulder to Jack. "George's grandson. I remember you as a little guy."

Jack stepped forward and extended his hand. "I remember you as well. Nice to see you again."

Rachel stepped aside as her mom shook Jack's hand.

"You're all grown up. I see why Rachel wants to spend so much time with you lately."

"Mom," Rachel murmured. "I'm just helping out."

Her mom had the audacity to wink at her before her focus went back to Jack. "Well, it's great to have you in town. I'm sure George would be so proud of the nice young man you've become."

The muscle in Jack's jaw ticked as he dropped his arm and nodded. Rachel wondered if emotions were getting to him. He couldn't escape the memory of his grandfather between the farm and the store. But she highly doubted Jack was one to discuss his feelings, especially with virtual strangers.

"How about the two of you come to dinner this weekend?"

Rachel stilled at her mother's proposal. Granted, Rachel had already told him about family dinner, but she didn't realize her mother would be so bold. Though Rachel wasn't surprised. Sarah Spencer was the quintessential hostess.

"I'm not sure—"

"We'll be there." Rachel cut off whatever excuse Jack was about to give. "And Jack has a potato salad request."

Her mother's eyes widened, as did her sweet smile. "Well, I can certainly make that happen."

The chime sounded again as another customer came through the old doors. Before Rachel could greet them, Myles came out from the back.

"Good morning," the teen stated. "Welcome to All Good Things. Is there anything I can help you with?"

Rachel noticed Jack turned to watch the interaction. The customer asked about cedar shavings for their landscaping to deter late-summer pests. Myles promptly motioned for the customer to follow as he led the way toward the appropriate aisle.

"He's a hard worker," her mother muttered.

"He is," Rachel agreed.

"Well, I'll let you two get back to work." Her mother smiled. "I just wanted to see my girl and bring her some goodies."

Rachel held up the plate. "I'll be sure to share."

Sarah moved forward and pulled Jack into a brief yet no doubt hearty embrace. "It's just so good to have you in town again. You definitely favor your grandfather."

She turned and walked out, leaving Rachel and Jack with the homemade treats.

"Let me put these in the office and then we'll continue the tour," she told him.

"Aren't you going to eat one?" he asked, following.

Rachel laughed. "Of course I am, and so are you. Nobody can turn down Sarah Spencer's kitchen creations. Trust me."

They each took a muffin top and left the rest in the office as Rachel continued the tour of the store. Jack took his notes and Rachel loved each time he asked a question because he wanted to learn more.

Rachel's cell vibrated in her pocket and she pulled it out and noticed not only the message, but also how late in the day it had got. Her father was asking if she'd be able to help him in the main barn for about an hour.

"I'm sorry." Rachel turned to Jack. "I'm going to need to head back to the farm."

"Don't be sorry," he told her. "This has been a huge help for me to understand this lifestyle better. I'll walk you out."

As they made their way into the hallway leading to the

back door, Rachel's cell vibrated again, but this time it was a call from her mother. Rachel swiped the screen as she followed Jack toward the exit.

"Hey, Mom. What's up?"

"I didn't want to say too much in front of Jack, but I'm so excited for you to bring him to dinner," her mom all but squealed. "A new boyfriend is so exciting."

Rachel froze at the back door and clutched her cell as she met Jack's confused gaze. "First, Jack is not my boyfriend. He's a friend passing through town."

"Same thing, dear," her mother went on. "I saw how you two tried not to stare at each other. That speaks volumes, so we need to make this a special occasion."

Rachel pinched the bridge of her nose and prayed for patience.

"You haven't brought a boy to dinner since Tyler."

Rachel pushed the old wooden door open and stepped into the sunshine, still willing that patience from above. She never thought her family would think Jack was *that* important. Of course he was important, but they weren't dating or anything else. Just because she still had a flutter in her belly after his hand touched hers last night… Such a simple gesture, innocent and sweet, yet she'd felt the warmth all the way to her heart.

He'd made no promises and had been very clear he had no intentions of staying. She knew what was happening, yet she couldn't stop herself from being drawn to him.

"I haven't brought a boy since Tyler because I haven't dated anyone," she said in a low voice.

"Well, we'll see where things go. Let's do a meal tonight instead of this weekend," her mom stated. "I'll see you both at six."

When the call disconnected, Rachel laughed at the way

her mom informed her instead of asking. And that was how Sarah Spencer earned respect and got things done.

Rachel headed toward her truck parked in the alleyway, but Jack had walked on ahead. She stopped short when she spotted a cat curled up next to her wheel. Jack bent down and was trying to coax it away from the vehicle.

Stray cats weren't uncommon around town, but she'd never had one cozy up next to her tire before. The dark gray animal seemed to be more kitten than full-grown cat. He had a paw curled in and was licking it over and over.

"He seems pretty comfortable here," Jack told her as she came to stand beside him.

When she unlocked her truck and opened the door, she assumed the cat would get scared and dart away, but it just kept licking its paw.

"Go on," she shooed. "I need to leave."

Jack chuckled and reached for the cat. He cradled it in the most adorable way against his dark shirt. He was going to be covered in hair, and she wondered if she should offer the lint roller she kept in her console.

"I think he's hurt."

Jack's concerned tone pulled her closer to the animal and Rachel noted the way the little paw curled in as the cat continued to lick. Rachel reached forward, still amazed at how gentle Jack was with this adorable cat.

"Oh, no. He does look hurt," Rachel agreed. "Let me wrap him up and I'll take him to my sister."

The amber cat eyes came up to hers and she saw the pain. She loved animals of all types and couldn't stand to see any hurt. Thankfully she knew the right person to help.

Rachel went to the cab of her truck and grabbed a hoodie from the passenger seat. She came back and wrapped the cat, careful of the injury. Jack handed the animal over with such a delicate manner that Rachel's heart melted a bit more. As if she needed another reason to fall for this man who wasn't staying.

"I'll take him straight to Violet," she repeated. "Do you want to stay and watch over Myles?"

"I can do that."

"And my mom changed dinner to six tonight," she remembered as she laid the cat on the passenger seat. "See you then."

"I'll be there," he assured her with an affirmative nod.

Rachel started up her truck as Jack closed her door. She didn't even bother texting her sister. She would be at the clinic in less than two minutes. Rosewood Valley wasn't large by any means, and the actual "town" part only had one main road that ran parallel to the park. Directions were easy, and even newcomers couldn't get lost here.

Thankfully the parking lot wasn't packed, but Rachel still pulled to the side door where the employees went in. She gathered the kitten back up and used the passcode to let herself inside. Barking and phones ringing immediately hit her. The place always seemed to be bustling with patients, and Violet wouldn't have it any other way.

Her younger sister had a knack for treating both animals and people with tender care.

"Oh, hey, Rachel."

She turned to find a familiar face heading down the hallway. "Callie, I'm so glad you're working today. I found this hurt cat behind the feed store."

Callie took the animal and nodded. "Follow me. I'll put you guys in this back room and go see if Vi is done with her current patient."

"I don't want to cut in line if others are waiting," Rachel stated.

Callie shook her head, sending her fiery red ponytail swaying. "No worries. We're slow at the moment."

She laid the cat on a metal exam table and turned around. "Wait here. Let me go get Vi."

Rachel took her place by the cat and waited on her sister to come in, which only took a few minutes. Vi swept in the door with her hair piled in a knot on top of her head and wearing a pair of red scrubs.

"Find a stray?" her sister asked.

Rachel nodded, but remained next to the table as Violet went to the other side.

"Behind the feed store. He's hurt his paw, but I didn't look for any other injuries."

Violet eased the hoodie away to examine the kitten. With her delicate hands, she felt around while the animal's eyes stared up.

"I hear we're having a guest for dinner tonight," Violet murmured as she lifted the injured paw. "Jack, who I am not allowed to call a boyfriend, according to Mom."

Rachel groaned. "Mom called you?"

"Texted," Violet corrected, then met Rachel's gaze. "Jenn, Luke, Paisley and Erin, too."

Rachel didn't know if she should cancel or tell Jack to run fast and far. But she'd never disrespect her parents that way. Still, it felt like she was throwing Jack to the wolves. Although she was rather impressed at the hotline her mother seemed to have with the rest of the family, considering she'd told them the plans and they'd only been changed about twenty minutes ago.

"I should've told her to keep it just Jack, Mom, Dad and me."

Violet laughed. "We'll be on our best behavior with your not-boyfriend."

Rachel started to respond, but Violet shifted back to work mode.

"There's a small laceration, but I don't think anything is broken."

"That's good," Rachel replied. "Do you have a place you can keep this kitty until we find him a home?"

Vi quirked a brow. "Oh, you're the home now. Don't you know that's how it works?"

Rachel shook her head. "Very funny. I don't have the time to care for a pet. You know my schedule on the farm and now with helping Jack. Surely you know someone who has a kid who would love a cuddly pet."

"Your lack of time is no excuse," Vi retorted with a grin. "Cats are easy. Leave them some empty boxes to sleep in and play with, keep their litter fresh, and have food and water. Pretty simple."

It wasn't that Rachel didn't want an animal. She lived on a farm. Animals were her life. She just didn't have the mental capability to care for anything else right now. She'd tapped out for the time being. She needed to live by her mother's motto of pouring into yourself before you could pour into others. Sarah Spencer had even bought each of her girls a gold chain with a white pitcher charm to remind them of this. If they didn't take care of themselves, how could they be the hands and feet of God?

"You can keep him for now," Violet stated, clearly not taking no for an answer.

Rachel sighed. "I don't know why I bothered arguing."

"Me, either. Now, I'm going to give you some ointment to put on his paw twice a day for a week. Let me go get that, and when I come back, I want to know about Jack."

Left alone with the kitten, Rachel had no idea how her

day had gone from making a simple thank-you dinner for Jack after he'd read her paper, to having him meet the entire family and gaining a new pet.

Chapter Nine

Jack brought his car to a stop at the Spencer home and glanced at the other vehicles. He'd been a little surprised that the dinner had been moved to tonight, but it wasn't like he had plans, so this was fine. Besides, when she'd dropped that bomb on him, she'd been so worried about the cat, he wasn't about to question anything. The animal's care had to come first.

All the other guests who seemed to be here did give him pause, though. He hadn't expected such an ordeal, but he wasn't going to be rude or disrespectful and cancel last minute.

He wasn't sure if he was about to come for an interrogation or what was going on. The only thing he knew was he'd had that delicious muffin top Sarah had made, and once Rachel left with the cat, he'd stuck around the feed store a bit longer before he'd had to meet with his contractor. He wished she'd given him a heads-up if the whole family was here, but there was no fixing that now.

It was time to really get this renovation ball in motion. After much consideration, he'd decided to leave a good bit of the home's charm like Rachel had suggested. He'd update the bathrooms and make the kitchen more efficient, but overall, there would be more cosmetic fixes than anything else.

Now that he had a clear picture of what was to be done and a proposed end date, he'd called a local homeless shelter to donate old clothing and some of the furniture that didn't have sentimental value. Now he just had to figure out what to do with those sentimental items. His father hadn't shown any interest in claiming them, so Jack assumed if anything was kept, it would be going home with him.

As he stepped from the car, Rachel came walking from the direction of her loft apartment. She had that signature side braid falling over one shoulder, a pair of worn jeans, cowgirl boots and a fitted cream-colored sweater to ward off the chill from the late-summer evening. The wholesome yet adorable style she had made him smile.

"So I need to confess something," she stated as she closed that distance between them. "My whole family is inside."

He offered a smile because she looked like she was ready to turn and bolt in the direction she'd just come from. "I can't wait to meet them," he assured her.

"No." Rachel shook her head and blew out a sigh. "I mean, like, the whole family. My three sisters, my soon-to-be brother-in-law and his niece, plus my parents."

He'd assumed as much from the whole drive full of cars, but knowing so many people waited just on the other side of the door did have a little bit of panic racing through him. The dinners he usually attended were with associates or potential clients. He had no clue how to handle a large, loving family and never really thought he'd find himself in this position.

"Your silence is concerning."

Jack reached out and laid his hand on her shoulder.

"I'm just processing. The largest dinners I've been to have been business meetings."

She scrunched her little nose. "I should've warned you when I found out earlier, but I was afraid you wouldn't come."

"To a homemade meal?" he scoffed. "I wouldn't miss it."

"You sure?"

After a reassuring squeeze, Jack dropped his hand and gestured toward the house. "Let's go. I can't wait to meet the crew. I barely remember your dad and sisters."

"You're a good sport," she commented. "My mom's rhubarb pie will be worth all of the chaos you're about to endure."

"You're not selling this evening well at all," he joked as they made their way up the wide gravel drive and around toward the back door. "It's like you want me to run in the other direction."

"Just warning you. This is your last chance."

He took her hand and gave a gentle squeeze before letting her go. "I'll be fine and so will you. Just relax."

Rachel stopped at the top of the steps and reached for the door handle before throwing a glance over her shoulder.

"It's hard to relax when my mother thinks you're my boyfriend."

Before he could reply, Rachel opened the door and stepped inside. He couldn't leave now, but why on earth would her mother think they were in a relationship? Jack had heard Rachel address that earlier on the phone, but then he'd got sidetracked by the injured cat and forgotten about it.

The moment Jack stepped into the screened-in back porch, the delicious mixture of scents hit him and he almost forgot Rachel's words, too. The chatter from apparently the entire family, the laughter echoing from the kitchen, was all so new to him, he wondered if he shouldn't go ahead and turn around.

But he'd never disrespect the Spencer family. They'd extended the invite, and surely he could endure one evening with a loving, close-knit family. Just because he didn't have experience with such things didn't mean he wouldn't enjoy himself…he hoped.

"Oh, you're here."

Sarah Spencer, donned in a yellow apron, rushed over to him with arms wide open. He found himself in a tight hug before she eased back with her hands on his shoulders. This was the second hug by this woman today, and he had to admit, the simple gesture left him feeling warm and welcome…like family.

"I'm so happy you came!" she exclaimed. "Rachel hasn't had anyone here since Tyler."

"Mom." Rachel's groan only caused laughter from her mother.

"I know. I'm just happy to have you guys here," Sarah went on. "George was such a special neighbor and we can't wait to catch up with his grandson."

The love his grandfather had for him had always been evident to him. But the more he hung around this town and the people, the more he realized just how special a man George truly was.

"Honey, let the man breathe. He just got here."

Will Spencer stepped into the kitchen and crossed the space to his wife. George always spoke so highly of Will, and Jack knew the two had been friends for years. He imagined them sharing a great many stories about farm life and family.

"Glad you could join us," Will greeted him. "Nothing

more my wife loves than a reason to have all her girls and our growing family under one roof."

"I'm Paisley." A little girl with purple glasses and a matching bow around her ponytail came bouncing up. "You're really tall," she added.

Jack laughed and squatted down. "It's nice to meet you. I hear you're going to be in a wedding soon."

She bobbed her head and smiled, revealing a few missing teeth. "Toot and Jenn are getting married and I get to wear a purple dress."

"I have a feeling that might be your favorite color," he replied, then stood back up. "So, who is Toot?"

The only man other than Will and Jack waved a hand. "You can call me Luke. P always calls me Toot because when she was younger she couldn't say 'Luke.' It's stuck and does seem confusing at times."

"Nice to meet you," Jack told him. "You're marrying Jenn? Right?"

Luke nodded and wrapped an arm around Jenn's waist. She leaned into him with a smile that so resembled Rachel's. But it didn't incite the same spark in him that Rachel's did. He shook Jenn's hand and glanced at the other sisters, who also shared that smile and those green eyes. They were clearly related, but there was something different about each one that made them unique.

"I'm Erin." The shortest sister, with her hair down in curls, stepped forward and extended her hand. "I hope you like chaos."

He chuckled and shook her hand. "Funny, that's how Rachel described this, too."

Jack turned his attention to the sister over by the oven taking out a casserole dish. She had her hair piled on top of her head, and once she set the dish on top of the stove, she turned to meet his gaze.

"You must be Violet," he greeted her.

She nodded. "That's me. I know you're not a boyfriend, but we're really glad you weren't scared off from a big family dinner."

Oh, he was scared all right, but he wasn't a coward and didn't run from a challenge. Besides, being in this room with everyone didn't make him want to turn and run. Surprisingly he felt as if he was in the midst of one gigantic hug. And he couldn't recall when he'd felt that way before.

"Can I do anything to help?" he offered, not really knowing what else to say or do with so many sets of eyes on him.

"You and Rachel can go have a seat in the dining room," Sarah told him. "We can bring everything in."

He might not know how family dinners worked, but he knew manners and he wasn't one to sit and watch while everyone else handled things.

Jack shook his head and moved around the island toward the empty glasses on the counter. "How about I fill these?" he offered.

Will whistled beneath his breath. "You're a brave man for not taking orders from my wife."

Jack glanced around the room and it seemed everyone was shocked. When his attention turned to Sarah, he found her smiling.

"I like him. Helpful and a gentleman." She winked at Rachel. "Maybe you can slide him into that boyfriend slot after all."

Jack couldn't help but laugh at her tenacity. He saw where Rachel got her bold and determined personality.

"I'm just doing the tea," he replied, reaching for one

of the pitchers. "I'll be heading back to San Francisco in just over a month."

"Then you have to come to the wedding."

Jenn's statement had him pausing. A family wedding was much more personal than a family dinner. He couldn't flat-out refuse, though he didn't feel comfortable crashing such an intimate family moment, so he did the only thing he could think of. He looked to Rachel for help.

Jack looked like he wanted to flee, so Rachel took pity on the poor guy and offered up a reply.

"I thought you wanted to keep the guest list small," she stated, giving her sister *the look* to stop pushing.

Jenn lifted a shoulder. "I do, but what's one more? We'd love to have you, Jack."

"I'll see what I can do," he told her.

Rachel needed to change the subject to not only get the heat off Jack, but also remove any question that they were anything more than friends or business associates at this point.

Regardless of how she felt in her heart, regardless of the fact she wished she could explore more with him, she had to face the harsh reality that he wasn't staying and his lifestyle was no different from her ex's. Why did she have to keep falling for men who didn't have that sticking factor?

Jack was so different from Tyler, though. Yes, he was a workaholic and worried about making money. But he had a heart for this place and the animals. He seemed genuinely interested, and there were times she was convinced he might talk himself into staying. She knew he'd enjoyed their ride and the peaceful moment they'd had at the pond.

But the fact remained that Rachel would want a partner in her farm life. While Jack seemed interested, this certainly wasn't the lifestyle he was used to.

"So I'm the proud new owner of a cat."

She really didn't know what to say, but she needed to change the subject and that was the most exciting thing in her life at the moment. Her family still didn't know about her online degree and they didn't know about the feed store issues she was helping Jack figure out.

So that left the stray cat.

"Did you remember the ointment before you came over?" Vi asked.

Rachel reached for a couple of the glasses Jack had filled and started toward the dining room. "I did," she confirmed. "And left the box and food and water just like you told me."

Violet grabbed glasses as well and followed. "And did you name him yet?"

"No. We're not getting that attached," Rachel said.

Jenn laughed from the dining room and called in, "That's what I thought and now I'm the proud owner of Cookie."

Jenn had come back to town and found a dog, a fiancé, and became a mother figure in record time. Rachel wasn't quite that far along in her life, but there wasn't a reason to name the cat. She'd find the animal a proper owner as soon as she had time. But for now, she'd care for him as best she could.

At Vi's gesturing, she and her sister grabbed more glasses and placed them on the dining table, passing Jenn as she crossed back to the kitchen. "So how serious are you and Jack?" Vi whispered once they were alone.

The bustle and chatter from the kitchen covered anything Rachel would want to reply, but she had to go with the truth and not her daydreams.

"We're just friends," Rachel assured her sister. "He's only here to sell the farm and possibly the feed store."

Violet's brows shot up. "And you're trying to get the house, right?"

"Trying, but I don't know if anything will work." More truth she couldn't deny. "He has reasons he needs to flip and sell quickly, and you know my financial situation."

"Well, he wouldn't have come to family dinner if he didn't like you, so I'm sure there's something stronger than a friendship there."

Rachel set the glasses down and shook her head. "Don't read anything into this. I thought Mom and Dad were going to be the only ones here until you told me otherwise. I'm sure Jack would've politely declined had I given him a proper heads-up."

"From the way that man was looking at you, don't bank on it." Violet's smile widened as she winked. "I'd say you have a little more control than you think."

The way he was looking at her? What did that mean? Did Violet see something that Rachel hadn't noticed? Her mother had hinted at something as well, so what was her family seeing?

"I wouldn't use an attraction to get favors," Rachel whispered since family started to filter in. "I need to do something to make everything fair for both of us. I'm just not sure what that is yet."

The moment Jack stepped through the arched doorway, his dark gaze met hers. That familiar flutter in her belly seemed to be a default feeling that accompanied his stare. The longer he remained in town, the deeper he got into her soul…into her heart.

"Go ahead and have a seat."

Sarah Spencer came in carrying one dish while Will

carried another. Luke brought a casserole and Paisley held a basket of rolls. Once the meal was presented on the table, Rachel took a seat and Jack came to sit next to her. Her parents took their spots at each end of the long farm table, which her mother had had made specifically in the hopes that her girls would marry and their crew would expand.

"This is just so perfect," her mother stated, clasping her hands. "I hope I made enough of everything."

"This is more food than I've seen on a table since my grandmother made Thanksgiving." Jack chuckled. "I appreciate you having me, but I hope this wasn't too much trouble."

"Trouble?" Rachel's mother waved her hand. "I love to cook and I love my family under one roof. You were a great excuse, and we're happy you're in town. I hear Rachel is helping you with the renovations and working a bit at the feed store."

"I wouldn't be able to do either without her," Jack assured them.

Her heart warmed once again. "I'm sure you'd be fine, but I'm glad I could be here for you."

Rachel's father reached for her hand. "Let's pray for our meal and then we can discuss the Circle H."

Everyone around the table joined hands, and the moment she reached for Jack's, her heart kicked up another notch. She'd been so used to this common family tradition, but from the look on Jack's face, he had no clue what was going on.

As her father said the prayer, Rachel gave Jack's hand a gentle squeeze. When he returned the gesture, she had a difficult time focusing on her father thanking God for all their blessings. She wanted to be that supportive friend for Jack and knew she was his main anchor in town. There was a line she simply couldn't cross no matter how much her heart was telling her to do just that.

Her father ended with an "Amen," and she released Jack's hand. Immediately the dishes were passed around and the family chatter commenced once again. She stole a glance toward Jack and noted for the first time since she'd known him that he looked absolutely terrified. She took the bowl of potato salad and lifted a spoonful.

"Here," she leaned in and whispered. "Start eating and you won't feel obligated to join in."

He blinked and shifted his eyes her way. "Thanks."

Once their plates were full, Rachel wanted to keep the mood off interviewing Jack.

"Other than shopping for our dresses this weekend, what else is left for the wedding?" she asked, meeting Jenn's gaze across the table.

"Honestly, nothing. That's why we wanted something small and just here on the farm." Jenn slathered a pat of butter on her homemade roll. "The ladies from the Women's Missions at church are doing the food in lieu of a gift, which is perfect. I don't need anything for my house anyway."

"Are the contractors still on time?" Rachel asked.

"Surprisingly they're ahead of schedule," Luke replied. "With the dry weather we've had, they were able to get everything under the roof sooner than expected, so the interior is nearly finished."

The low hum of a vibrating phone caught Rachel's attention, and Jack slid his hand into his pocket and pulled out his phone. Rachel didn't miss the name on the screen, even though Jack tried to hold his device beneath the table so as not to be rude.

"I'm sorry," he stated as he eased his chair back. "Excuse me while I take this. It's my father."

"Of course," Rachel's mom said.

Rachel didn't miss the worry in Jack's eyes as he stepped from the room. She heard him answer, but nothing after the back door opened and closed. Rachel didn't know the dynamics of that father-son relationship, but she knew enough to know there wasn't anything warm and cozy.

While wedding and house discussions went on around her, Rachel tried to concentrate on the delicious meal and not what Jack was dealing with regarding his father.

Moments later he stepped back in, his face impassive. Whatever had taken place with that phone call had put a look on his face she'd never seen before.

He took his seat next to her once again and she leaned over.

"You okay?"

He paused a minute before quietly saying, "Not really."

Rachel knew that admission cost him. He had his pride and he was a strong man. Whatever his father had said had knocked the wind from Jack's sails. Not only that, but this was also a much-needed dose of reality to remind her that Jack was only here for one purpose...and it wasn't to fall in love and live happily ever after as a farmer.

Chapter Ten

He'd stayed long enough to not be disrespectful or rude. Dinner tasted amazing, as did the homemade pie, and the potato salad was exactly how he remembered. Jack probably would've enjoyed the whole evening even more if only he'd ignored that call from his father. He should've let it go to voicemail and then he could've been in the moment with the Spencer clan instead of smiling and trying to fit in with the small talk after the news from his father.

He let himself in the back door of the Hart farmhouse and flicked on the light to the kitchen. He set his keys on the island and maneuvered his way around a stack of boxes he'd brought down from the upstairs bedrooms.

The emotions whirling around inside him couldn't be described, not when they were all over the place. Hurt, confusion, anger...betrayal.

The tap on his back door had Jack turning around and suppressing a sigh. He should've known she'd follow him back home. Rachel wasn't dumb, and she worried about those she cared for. And as much as he just wanted to be alone in his misery, he wouldn't turn her away or be impolite to the one true friend he had at the moment.

Jack maneuvered around the boxes once again and slid the lock open. The moment he stepped aside, Rachel let herself in and closed the door behind her. She tipped her head and those worry lines deepened between her brows.

"You don't have to tell me what happened at dinner if you don't want," she started. "But I'm a pretty good listener and I feel I owe you for all the whining I've done to you."

"You haven't whined one bit," he corrected. "And I'm happy to listen to you anytime."

She reached out and placed a hand on his arm. That tender touch calmed him and he found himself taking a deep breath. There was nothing he could do right now or even tomorrow. He had to move ahead with his plans just like he'd been doing. He still had a goal within his reach and every intention of obtaining it.

Jack blew out a sigh and turned to get out of the congested area by the back door.

"What are all the boxes?" she asked, following him into the den.

He pointed toward the now bare built-in shelves. "Nearly all the books from in here and several things from the guest rooms upstairs. Artwork and knickknacks. I haven't found too much that I'd want to keep, and anything I do keep, I have no clue where it will go."

He moved over to the desk and tapped his fingertips on the scarred top.

"I can still see him sitting in here," Jack murmured, staring at the old leather chair. "He'd go over his livestock and the trading he'd do with other farmers. He'd study rain patterns and droughts and read all the history to figure out the future of farming. I never understood half the stuff he talked about, but he'd tell me like I was going to be the one to take the reins one day."

Rachel's boots clicked on the hardwoods behind him, then muffled as she stepped onto the area rug. He didn't turn around, didn't want to remove himself from the memories.

"I remember him sitting behind this desk when Grandma passed away," Jack went on. "The only time I saw him cry. He wondered how he'd go on living here without her. I never really understood the love between a man and a woman until that moment. My mother passed away when I was little. I don't even remember her. My dad doesn't date, or if he does, he keeps it quiet. He's all in with his work, so that's all I know."

Jack turned to face her, finding her closer than he'd thought. She had that concerned look once again…or somewhere between pity and concern. He didn't want pity, but he knew that was just Rachel's giving heart.

"I see how your family all just meshes together and that's so odd to me," he went on, then shook his head. "That didn't come out right and I didn't mean to sound ungrateful or insulting."

"I didn't take it that way," she assured him. "My family is loud at times and we love hard. If that's not something you're used to, I can see how it would be overwhelming. I promise I only found out a little before dinner about the whole crew."

"Don't apologize for having an amazing family." He didn't want her to be sorry for anything when clearly he had some things to work through. "You were fortunate and I didn't realize what I was missing until I got that call and my world came crashing into yours."

"Was the call from your father?" she asked.

Jack nodded. As much as he didn't want to get into this, he owed Rachel an explanation for not staying longer and for mentally checking out of the dinner with her family. They had all tried to include him in the conversation and made him feel so welcome. Maybe that was what had him so cranky now. His father had interrupted one of the purest, most enjoyable moments Jack could remember. Rachel's family didn't expect anything from him. They had all seemed genuinely interested in what he was doing to the house and his plans for the feed store. Not once was money mentioned or who would be his top-dollar buyer.

"I'm sorry he upset you." Rachel's soft tone pulled him from his thoughts.

"I don't even know if I'm upset," he stated honestly. "Angry, frustrated, maybe annoyed. I guess *upset* is a good blanket term for all the emotions my father evokes."

"Why do you let him do that to you?" she asked, her brows drawn in as she took another step closer.

Confused, Jack asked, "Excuse me?"

"If you get so angry, why don't you remove yourself from a situation that will cause so many negative emotions?"

Remove himself? How on earth could he just remove himself from his father's life? They worked together—they were really all the family either of them had left.

"I don't mean ignore him," she corrected. "I'm saying put some distance between you, and try to focus on what makes you happy. When was the last time you did something for yourself that had nothing to do with work or your father?"

Jack took a moment and tried to think of his life lately. He'd been so focused on getting those few house renovations set, and now trying to figure out the missing money from the store, he hadn't done much for himself.

Except that ride.

"I went out with you on the horses around the farm and the pond," he finally told her. "That was fun and had nothing to do with work."

Her face relaxed as her lips lifted into a soft smile. "We did have fun and I think you even let your mind take a rest for a bit."

"I did. Must be the company I've been keeping."

He sat on the edge of the desk and laced his fingers together as he continued to stare back at her. Rachel was the type of person who could make a man want to open his heart fully. The type who wouldn't judge but would listen and try to put your needs ahead of her own.

No, she wouldn't try—she *would* put others' needs ahead of her own. She'd already proved that by helping at the store. Granted, he was paying her and she wanted to get this property, but she didn't have ulterior motives. Rachel Spencer was one of the most honest and trustworthy people he knew.

"My father called to inform me that Brian has been working out of the new office," Jack explained. "The office that wasn't supposed to be open to the public until after the promotion decision was made." His stomach clenched as he recalled the phone call earlier.

"Brian is the other guy up for this position?" she asked.

Jack nodded. "Dad has always considered him another son. He applied to the firm straight out of college, so we started about the same time. Dad tried to mold both of us, but Brian has my father's work ethic and mindset. Their lives are all about money. Maybe he would've been a better son for my father. They are similar in the way they think and will do anything to make a sale. Sometimes I wonder why I'm trying so hard."

"Because you want your only family member to be proud of you," she explained. "And there's nothing wrong with that. But when you're not appreciated for the work you're doing or constantly trying to prove yourself, then maybe you need to reevaluate why you started this work in the first place."

Jack glanced down at his hands, not quite sure what to say at this point. Rachel seemed to have the right words and the perfect understanding tone for Jack to wonder if he should be doing something different. But what? He'd never known anything else in his life, and he'd been climbing that invisible ladder for years.

"If you love real estate, that's great. But make sure you're doing it for you and not because it's expected." She reached for his joined hands and covered them with hers. "Does that make sense?"

Jack turned his hands over in hers, wanting to feel that connection and draw from her amazing strength.

"I've never thought of my career as doing something I love," he replied. "I'm good at it, so that's all I know. But I do enjoy what I'm doing. I meet all sorts of people and help them find the perfect home or business."

"You're making dreams come true. That has to feel good."

He couldn't help but smile at her outlook. "You think of things in ways I never would have."

She lifted a slender shoulder. "Because I'm on the outside with fresh eyes looking in. You're submerged in this life."

"Have you ever thought of becoming a therapist?" He chuckled. "If the farm life doesn't work for you."

"There's nothing else I'd rather do with my life."

She eased her hands from his and slid them into the back of her jean pockets, but she didn't step away and her eyes never wavered from his.

"So, what can we do to make this better?" she asked. "We can come up with a way for you to tell your dad how he's making you feel or we can put that topic to rest for the night. Whatever you need, I'm here."

Why did he have a feeling she'd always be there for him? Even when his time in Rosewood Valley came to an end and he went back home, he knew without a doubt that he could always call on her.

"Let's table this discussion," he told her. "Dad has sucked enough of my mental energy out for one day."

With a curt nod, Rachel glanced around the room. "I hope there's no change planned in here."

"None," he said, pushing off the desk. "Well, the built-ins could use a sand job and fresh stain. I decluttered but the rest of the furniture and rug will stay for staging. I definitely want the desk, though. Not sure where I'll put it, but that piece is important to me."

Rachel turned back to him. "Does your father want anything from the house?"

"He's never shown interest or asked what I was doing with the contents, so I have to assume he doesn't."

"When are the contractors starting?" she asked.

"Monday, and they claim they'll be done in three weeks."

"That's good." She moved toward the built-ins on either side of the fireplace. "I'm not giving up on getting this place, just so you know. I can't be this close to my goal and watch it all slip away."

The ball of guilt tightened in his gut. He had the exact same thoughts on his end. He had his own goals, and this house would be the final step to reach everything he'd been working for. At least, he had to hold on to that promise. Just because Brian was working from the new office didn't mean anything. He hadn't been given the title or the lead.

Selling this farm would prove so much. Not only would this be his biggest sale of the year, but knowing he could market and successfully find a buyer in an area outside of his wheelhouse would prove to his father that he could do more than sell just inside the city.

"I get where you're coming from," he offered.

After trailing her fingers over the spine of his grandfather's Bible, she shifted back around. "There has to be another way to get your promotion where I can get this land."

Jack said nothing; she'd already figured out his predicament and he honestly couldn't see a way for them both to have what they wanted.

"Okay, then." Rachel blew out a sigh of frustration that matched his current mood. "That's quite a stumbling block, but I have faith. God didn't lead me through all of this with my family for me to end up with nothing."

Her faith astounded him. She didn't get flustered; she just kept moving forward. While his mindset told him to keep moving toward his own goal, his heart had started pulling him in the opposite direction.

"It's getting late. I should go. I just wanted to check on you and make sure you were okay."

Rachel started toward the door and he wanted her to stay, but for what? He could invite her to watch a movie or sit on the patio and enjoy the starry late-summer evening. But his emotions were all over the place where she was concerned, and he wasn't sure how to get them back under control…or if that was even possible at this point.

Jack crossed the room and replied, "You could've just texted me."

She stopped in the doorway and turned. "When someone I care about is hurting, I won't text."

He stopped directly in front of her and he couldn't ignore his attraction. Far beyond her physical attributes, she had an inner beauty that he'd never quite seen before. Each time they were together, he wanted to find more and more reasons to cling to the way she made him feel. A light inside him had been flipped on in the most unexpected way, but he had no idea what to do with his newfound emotions or if he should do anything at all.

"You're remarkable," he murmured.

Her smile had his heart doing another flip. "You've said that before, but thank you. I like to think you would've come to check on me if you knew I was sad."

She came up on her tiptoes and placed a soft kiss on his cheek.

"Good night, Jack."

For reasons he couldn't explain, he remained in the doorway while she let herself out. Her delicate touch warmed him, and he put his hand on his cheek like that moment shifted something inside him. How silly could he be? He and Rachel couldn't be more opposite, and they had entirely different goals…with this house being right between them.

Jack snapped out of his trance. He had a sinking feeling one or both of them would get hurt when he had to leave, because this property couldn't go in two different directions. He could either work a deal with Rachel and lose his promotion or he could stick with his plan and sell, leaving Rachel's dreams crushed.

Either way, someone was going to lose.

Chapter Eleven

❧

"The off-the-shoulder dress is stunning."

Rachel turned from side to side in the three-way mirror as she stood on the platform at the dress shop. She liked the strapless one she'd had on earlier, but Jenn loved this one, and since the wedding was for Jenn, Rachel didn't mind one bit.

She met Jenn's reflection in the mirror. "It's the perfect color," she told her. "I think it will match the flowers beautifully."

Sarah clasped her hands on the edge of the pale pink velvet sofa. "My girls are going to be stunning."

Rachel lifted the flowy skirt of her plum-colored dress and turned to her mother. "What about you? I saw your dress on and you are going to be the most breathtaking mother of the bride ever."

Her mother waved her hand and scoffed. "Oh, please."

"You think we'll get Dad out of those red suspenders?" Jenn asked, wrinkling her nose.

Their mother chuckled. "I had to make him a compromise. He could wear them beneath his suit jacket."

"He wouldn't be the same man without them," Rachel agreed.

Violet stepped out wearing the same dress as Rachel, and Rach had to admit the design did look romantic and elegant. The deep color would be perfect for the season and in the gardens on the farm.

"I love it," Vi stated. "And I don't need any alterations."

"I think I just need a hem," Rachel replied, fluffing out her skirt.

Erin slipped from behind a curtain and had on her own dress as well. They were doing the same color, but their own choice of style. She'd been the first one to dress before helping Paisley.

"Who's ready for the most beautiful flower girl to ever exist?" Erin asked, holding the curtain shut. "There are no alterations needed for this one, either. Just accessories and a great hairstyle."

"Let's see our girl!" Sarah exclaimed.

As they each turned to face the closed drape, Erin did a little drumroll with her lips as she slowly pulled the thick material aside to reveal Paisley. She came out of the dressing room in her own purple dress with her arms spread wide and did a spin, earning a clap and a few whistles.

"I love it," Paisley declared as she went toward the mirror. "I feel like a princess."

Rachel stepped off the platform to give Princess Paisley her shining moment. Violet and Erin came to stand behind the girl, and Jenn came up beside them.

"I will have the best wedding party in the world," Jenn exclaimed. "What kind of shoes do you want, Paisley?"

"Am I too young for a heel?"

"Not at all," Jenn replied. "I'm sure we can find something the perfect size for your age."

One of the young workers who had been helping them popped back in and the shoe hunt was on. Violet went to change from her dress and Erin went to help Jenn get some jewelry for Paisley.

Sarah Spencer patted the seat beside her as she looked up at Rachel. "Sit down for a minute."

Her mother wasn't asking, and Rachel knew when her mom had something on her mind. She gathered the material of her skirt and sank down onto the plush sofa.

"How's Jack?"

As always, her mother wasted no time getting to the point.

"He called the following day to thank me for dinner, but he seemed almost sad when he left that night," her mother went on.

Of course he'd called. Jack might be a business mogul from a big city, but he didn't lack manners and morals. They'd had dinner three days ago and she'd sent him some wallpaper links, but she'd been so busy with the farm and the feed store and school, she hadn't seen him.

And she missed him more than she should.

"He had gotten a call from his father during dinner," Rachel explained. "I don't know what all he's dealing with regarding his dad, but I don't think they have a healthy relationship."

"I assumed they didn't," her mother stated. "At least, if I had to guess. I remember Jack coming during the summers, but his dad rarely made an appearance. I know that always seemed to upset George, and I never asked, but figured there was a disconnect somewhere."

"I really don't know what happened, if the problem was with Jack's dad and grandfather or Jack's dad and Jack." Rachel pulled in a deep breath and tried to make sense of a situation she knew very little about. "I went to the farm after dinner because I could tell he was stressed. I just wish he'd let me help more than he is."

"You care quite a bit for him."

Rachel jerked back at her mother's bold statement, and none too quietly, either.

"He's a *friend*," Rachel insisted. "Of course I care."

"The best ones always start out in the friend category." Her mother patted Rachel's hand. "It's okay to admit you have feelings for him. He's a handsome young man with a nice personality, and he seemed to be quite taken with you."

How did everyone see something she didn't? What looks was Jack giving her for her family to be so in tune?

"Mom, don't get so excited," Rachel warned. "He's a friend that I am helping and he's going back home in about a month."

"A great many things can happen in a month."

Yes, they could, but she wasn't about to get her mother's hopes up. If Rachel started thinking in terms of something beyond a friendship with Jack, she'd get hurt, and she'd already been down that path. Another career-minded man who stole her heart and attention, another man who wasn't cut out for the farm life.

But everything about Jack seemed to be so different and completely…right.

Yet it wasn't. God wouldn't send someone who wasn't staying. The man who was meant to be for her would have her interests and share the love of this town.

"He's not like Tyler."

As if her mother could read her mind, her words broke into Rachel's thoughts.

"No, he's not," Rachel agreed. "But they do have some similarities."

"Not the ones that matter."

There was no arguing with Sarah Spencer once she made up her mind. Obviously her family liked Jack, and Rachel loved that he'd got along so well with everyone.

She would talk to him privately about attending the wedding, but she had to make it clear to her entire family that Jack was only a friend and temporary in town.

Rachel came to her feet and stared down at her mother. "I know you mean well, and I know you only want the best for me, but we have to be patient. And as much as I want a wedding day and a family of my own, I have to face the real possibility those things might not be in my future for a bit longer."

Her mother came to her feet and pulled Rachel into an embrace. Was there anything more comforting or loving than a mother's hug? Rachel returned the gesture and held tight for a moment.

"I know God has a special plan for you," her mom whispered. "He always looks out for His children."

Yes, He did. Rachel kept reminding herself of that, and honestly, she was beyond blessed. She had more than she'd ever need and well beyond anything she deserved. Her family farm had been saved, her sister was marrying the love of her life and bringing an adorable little girl into their world, and in less than a year, she would have her degree. Life was moving forward for everyone, maybe not the way Rachel had hoped, but forward in a positive direction nonetheless.

She prayed for Jack and the situation with his father. Maybe Jack coming to Rosewood Valley had nothing to do with her and everything to do with his personal and spiritual growth. And if her only part was to help him with his walk with God and his difficulties with his father, then so be it.

Jack stepped through the back door of All Good Things and inhaled the scent of grain and wood. The more he hung around town and this place, the more acclimated he became to country life. Maybe he didn't fully understand it all, but he did appreciate how hard people worked and how they all seemed to be supportive of each other. Small-town life was not only more laid-back than the city, but it also wasn't as competitive.

He'd yet to meet the manager, and he really needed to introduce himself. Now that the contractors were at the house, he needed reasons to step out and get out of their way. Always trying to hang with Rachel seemed odd, and a little pushy, since he'd made it clear they were friends and he had no intention of staying in town.

The thought of leaving didn't appeal to him like it had when he'd first come to town. Maybe he'd just got used to all the friendly people and the homey place. Or maybe there was one certain woman who had changed his entire thought process.

Regardless, he still had to move on with his plans, and the farmhouse was going to be absolutely amazing once those few rooms got a little facelift. He'd already ordered one of the wallpapers that Rachel had suggested for the main bath. He had to admit, she had a serious eye for design. Maybe farming was her passion, but she had many talents that she could tap into if she truly wanted some extra cash. He knew she wanted a place of her own, *his* place, but that wasn't likely. Still, she deserved something of her own, and he wanted to help her in any way he could.

For now, he had to deal with the feed store. Walt was back from his vacation, so this meeting had to be his top priority.

The office door was closed, but not latched. He tapped his knuckles on the door and waited for someone to call him in. Just because he was the owner didn't mean he didn't respect privacy. This place was more Walt's than Jack's and that was okay.

"Come in," a gruff voice called from the other side.

Jack eased the door open and stepped over the threshold. "Is this a bad time?"

An elderly man with silver hair and denim overalls covering his rounded belly came to his feet.

"Not at all if you're George's grandson."

Jack nodded. "I am. Thought it was time to introduce myself. Rachel has told me a good deal about you."

"Has she now?" Walt came around his desk and held out his hand for Jack. "She's told me about you as well. Gotta say, I thought your grandfather would live forever. He seemed to be a staple not just in the store, but also in the community."

"I've heard that." Jack shook Walt's hand, then released it and slid his thumbs through his belt loops. "I just wanted to let you know I haven't quite decided what I'm doing with this building yet. I had intentions of selling because I don't live here and have no need for a business, but I might just keep it and continue to let you manage. No matter what happens, I will make sure your job is secure. This place wouldn't be what it is without you, according to Rachel."

Walt gripped the straps on his overalls and rocked back on his heels. "That's not true. Your grandfather is the one who gets the praise. All I do is inventory and people managing. Nothing too hard. He did all the grunt work making a name for the place."

Jack couldn't help but accept the burst of pride that spread through him. The way people talked about his grandfather like he was some type of superhero to Rosewood Valley really had Jack wishing he would've spent more time here. While he appreciated all the summers he'd been here, he just wanted to have more memories stored up. Did he appreciate his grandfather enough? Did his grandfather know how much Jack loved him?

As he'd got older and into high school, sports and girls took up his time. Then Jack would call, but that also got few and far between. He just hoped his grandfather never doubted how much he meant to Jack. Now was his chance to honor the most remarkable man.

"I'd like to see what I can help with or if you have any concerns about the store in general."

Jack laid that out, hoping Walt would address the funds. Maybe he'd been doing his own investigation. While Walt might also be the one pilfering the money, Jack trusted Rachel when she said no way would something like that have happened. He also trusted his grandfather, and George Hart wouldn't have put someone in charge if they weren't trustworthy. But Jack wouldn't reveal what he knew quite yet.

"My biggest concern would be my job and my employees," Walt replied. "I want to do right by them. I'm old enough to retire, but I love what I do and will continue to work as long as the good Lord allows."

"I'm happy to hear that because I certainly couldn't keep this place running without you," Jack replied. "So, aside from that, is there anything else that concerns you? Anything with the staff or how well the store is doing as a whole?"

Walt hesitated and then let out a long sigh. "Close that door, would ya?"

A private conversation? Maybe they were getting somewhere.

Jack reached behind him and closed the door with a soft click before focusing on Walt again.

"What's up?" Jack asked, crossing his arms over his chest.

"I'm not sure what all you know about the store or how far you dug into things while I was on vacation," Walt began. Then he circled his desk and took a seat. "The store isn't bringing in what it used to when George was alive."

Jack moved closer to the desk and made himself comfortable in the old wooden folding chair opposite Walt. He'd let the guy take the lead here and reveal anything he knew or suspected.

"You think his passing caused the decline in sales?"

Walt rested his forearms on the desk and shook his head. "No. I'm afraid someone is taking money from the store. I don't want to just accuse anyone, and I don't have solid proof, but something is off over the past few months."

Jack eased forward just a bit in his chair. "When did you first notice money missing?"

"About a month ago I had a hunch something wasn't quite right with the numbers." Walt reached into a drawer and pulled out a folder. "And I've been looking over more things since I've been back and it's still quite troubling."

"Did you have a new hire about the time you started noticing an issue?"

Walt flipped open the cover of the folder and picked up the top paper. He turned it to face Jack and slid it across the desk. This wasn't something Jack had seen before. This paper was a spreadsheet that looked like something Walt had done up since his return. Jack was impressed, quite honestly. He didn't know if his grandfather would be one to do a spreadsheet. He'd always done old-school pen and paper and kept files secured in a cabinet.

As Jack glanced over the numbers, he saw a good bit of what he and Rachel had noticed.

"I've hired three new people and then you brought on Rachel just the other day," Walt stated. "Safe to say we can rule out Rachel."

"Pretty safe bet," Jack agreed.

Not only because of the timing, but also because he'd bet his annual salary there wasn't a corrupt bone in her body.

"I know the families of the ones I've hired and wouldn't think anyone would take from me," Walt went on. "But we can't ignore facts."

No, they couldn't.

"I'll be honest." Jack slid the paper across the desk and eased back in his chair. "I noticed some off-putting numbers when I first started looking at things. That's the main reason I asked Rachel to put in a few hours a week. I figured nobody would think anything of her being here, plus she's extremely knowledgeable."

"Smart move." Walt stuffed the paper back into the folder and put it back into his drawer. He leaned back in his creaky leather chair and laced his fingers over his belly. "I trust all of this will stay between the three of us."

"Absolutely," Jack promised. "And now with all of us on the lookout, we should be able to solve this quickly and quietly. I don't want the store or my grandfather's reputation tarnished in any way."

Walt studied him. "You're a good man. I don't think any of that will happen with you in charge. Your grandfather would be proud of the man you've become."

Would he? Jack hoped so, but he hadn't seen the man in a few years before his passing. That guilt weighed heavy on him, and perhaps that was why Jack was so torn on whether or not to keep the store or sell it. Having a link to his grandfather seemed right. Another way for Jack to keep his connection here in Rosewood Valley. Perhaps he needed a reason to return every now and then without it being so obvious he wanted to see Rachel.

What would happen when she finally found the one and settled down on her own? How would he feel then? Would he be happy for her or would he wonder if he'd let the greatest woman he knew slip away?

Chapter Twelve

Jack let himself in the front door since the construction crew was in the back working in the kitchen. A bit of the weight on his shoulders had lifted since talking to Walt. Jack had to agree with Rachel. That man had integrity and wouldn't do anything to harm the store.

He also felt a bit better knowing the house was on its way to getting on the market. Each step of progression put him that much closer to his own branch of the real estate firm. He couldn't wait to start his own legacy, something he could pass down to his children when the time came.

He vowed to be a more hands-on father, a more loving father. Yes, money was important, but from his short time here in Rosewood Valley, he could see that money was not the bottom line. Family had to come above all else.

The moment he crossed the threshold, he stopped.

"What are you doing here?"

Rachel turned a short white vase from side to side as she adjusted the various stems of colorful flowers. She flashed him that megawatt smile and any worries he had simply vanished.

"Oh, I wasn't sure when you'd be home and I rode Sunshine over so I could put this bouquet in your entryway." She stepped back and clasped her hands. "There. That's better."

Jack closed the door and chuckled. "You rode over on your horse with a vase of flowers?"

"I rode over with a bundle in my saddlebag," she corrected. "I found the vase in the storage closet here."

The banging of a sledgehammer had him jerking his attention toward the hallway leading toward the back of the house.

"Do you normally decorate while in a construction zone?" he asked.

Rachel turned and crossed her arms over her chest. "The foyer wasn't on the list, so I figured there needed to be one room that was completely done and cheery. I also went to school with your head contractor, so I brought the guys some biscuits with homemade apple butter."

Jack raked a hand through his hair. He'd never seen a woman with so much on her plate, yet still doling out favors and niceties to others.

"How's the kitchen looking?" he asked.

"Like a disaster. There will be no meals in there for a while, which is why I put something in the Crock-Pot for us back at my place."

Jack blinked, processing the words she'd just said. She'd started something for their dinner?

"I really don't know what to say," he admitted. "You know you don't have to feed me, right? I can go into town for something or make a sandwich."

Her mouth dropped as she gasped. "You will not be making a sandwich for your dinner. That's just ridiculous. You're not camping."

He couldn't stop his laugh now. "Is that when I should eat sandwiches? When I'm camping?"

"I'm just stating there's no reason to rough it when you

have a friend more than willing to cook. I have to eat, too," she explained with a shrug.

Friends. Yes. The term that summed up their relationship and one he needed to remember. But there were times he wondered if their situation would be different if he didn't have an established life and career somewhere else. If he didn't have things yet to prove, and goals he'd worked too hard to accomplish to abandon now. Would he come home from work and find her making their house cozy like she'd just done with the flowers? He would never expect his wife to do all the cooking, decorating and cleaning. He firmly believed in any relationship the responsibilities should be shared, but he had to admit having her greet him with that smile the moment he stepped through the door had his mind traveling down a path he couldn't keep ignoring.

"You're doing it again," she told him.

The hammering stopped and the guys in the back started discussing something he couldn't quite make out.

"What's that?" he asked.

"Staring like you want to say something but you don't know how."

She'd got that right. He did want to say something, but it wasn't that he didn't know how…more like he didn't know what to say. Did he say he was falling for this town? Did he admit he'd started feeling more for her than he'd anticipated? Then what? They'd both feel awkward because there was no future here. He didn't want her hurt, and she'd already had one guy walk away. He wouldn't be another man to break her heart. The pressure from his father to make this sale and get back to the brokerage weighed heavy on him. It had weighed heavier each day since their last phone call.

Which meant he had to suppress anything he felt, because his feelings were only going to grow if he focused on them.

"I'm just happy you're here," he told her honestly. "Thank you for the flowers."

"You're welcome. Heard you went by the feed store today."

He nodded. "Word travels fast in this town."

"Walt called me just a bit ago," she explained. "He said you guys discussed the issue, so I'm glad we're all going to be on top of this."

When the hammering started up again, Jack motioned for her to head upstairs. Once on the landing, the noise was a bit more muted.

"He said he'd been doing his own digging," Jack told her as he leaned against the railing. "He also told me he'd hired three people around the same time and he only noticed the missing funds about a month ago."

Rachel slid her hands into her pockets as she pursed her lips, clearly in thought. Her signature braid fell over her right shoulder, lying flat against her long-sleeve plaid shirt. She'd tucked her top into her jeans and had a brown belt that matched her brown boots. She was pure cowgirl through and through.

"It's just difficult to imagine any of his workers taking money," she murmured. "They all should know he'd give anything if they needed it."

Jack had no doubt Walt would do anything for anyone. That was just another aspect about this town that he loved. Everyone's willingness to step up without being asked or expecting something in return.

"I don't see any other explanation other than an employee," Jack stated.

"It would have to be," she murmured, glancing down. "And it's going to be devastating to whomever it is. It's a small town and people will talk. I just hate this."

There she went with that big heart again and her worries for everyone else, even if they were in the wrong.

"I just hope I figure out who it is first," she added, bringing her worried gaze back up to him. "Maybe then I can talk them into returning the money or something."

Yeah, he really had no clue how he and Walt would handle this once they found out who the culprit was. Stealing was wrong no matter what, but Jack couldn't help but wonder about the circumstances.

"So, when would you like to head over for dinner?" she asked. "I don't want to scare you away, but I did try a new recipe. So we could be ordering a pizza in the end."

Jack shrugged. "Fine by me. I'll eat whatever. Just let me talk to the guys downstairs first and change clothes."

"You're getting out of your businessman attire?" She nodded and gave a thumbs-up. "Nice. Can't wait to see what you dress down in."

Why did he have to find all sides of this woman appealing? The compassionate side, the giving side, and even her snarky sense of humor at his expense. He found every aspect of her adorable and much too attractive. She could make him laugh and feel things he hadn't in...well, maybe never.

"Very funny," he retorted with a mock laugh. "We'll see who's laughing once we try this mystery meal you made."

"It's not a mystery," she scoffed, barely hiding her grin with the twitch of her lips. "I know everything that's in it. I've just never done this one before."

"Give me about twenty minutes and I'll be there," he assured her. "I don't have a horse, so I'll be driving."

"You city boy." She started down the steps and called back, "See you in just a bit."

When she got to the first floor, she yelled toward the kitchen, saying her farewell to the workers. Jack always found himself in a better mood after being in Rachel's presence. Just as he started to head to the bedroom, the cell in his pocket vibrated. When he slid it out, he noticed his father's name. Jack's thumb hovered over the screen, but he didn't answer.

Never in his life had he not taken a call from his father, but right now, he was in such a good mood and he was ready to go see Rachel in a few minutes. He didn't want to be filled with anxiety and negativity.

Jack donned a pair of jeans and a long-sleeve T-shirt. He grabbed his sneakers and tied those up, too. There, now she shouldn't say anything, right?

Good grief. He truly was like a teen with a crush, all worried about his outfit and what she would think.

Jack wanted to see if the guys needed anything before he left, even though he assumed they had it all under control. He was excited to see the progress, even though with most things the rooms or buildings got worse before they got better. He knew in no time this place would be ready to sell.

And with that thought, the lump of guilt weighed heavy knowing he already had the perfect buyer…just not the one he could realistically sell to.

"This is so silly," Rachel muttered to herself as she took the lid off the Crock-Pot. "It's a meal. That's all."

The stray cat slid by her leg and Rachel jumped. She still wasn't used to having a pet, but she had to admit, she didn't feel as silly talking to herself with something else in the room.

The lasagna didn't look or smell terrible, but she'd never tried making it in a Crock-Pot. Her mother would not believe it. At least the sauce was homemade with tomatoes from their garden. That had to count for something. And the bread was homemade as well. So what if she'd cheated a little with using a slow cooker.

But it wasn't the meal she felt silly about. She'd made an impulsive purchase and now...well, she just had to go through with the gift giving. She didn't necessarily have extra funds right now, considering she wanted to buy a house, but she couldn't help herself. And like with most every other aspect in her life, she made the leap without thinking.

She had no idea who her guardian angel was, but Rachel had a feeling she followed her around shaking her head.

The tap on her door had Rachel spinning away from the kitchen and smoothing a hand down her braid. Should she have done something else with her hair? Something less boring?

Too late now. Jack was here and she had nerves curling through her belly like this was her first date. Only this wasn't their first date or any type of a date. It was a friendly meal where they could chat about their day, and maybe the store and renovations, and she could give him his present.

The cat scurried toward the bedroom as Rachel crossed to open the door. She blinked at the man standing before her.

"Well, you did pack casual clothes. I'm so proud of you." When he started to enter, she held up a hand. "Or did you go buy those when I laughed at all of your dressy clothes?"

"I packed them all by myself," he replied and tapped the tip of her nose with his finger. "Now, something smells amazing and I'm pretty hungry. Please tell me it turned out okay?"

She eased aside as he let himself in. "I haven't tried a sample yet, but it looks fine."

"Then it will be great," he assured her, then suddenly pulled his cell from his pocket.

He glanced to the screen and sighed before shoving it away.

"Everything okay?" she asked.

Offering her a small grin, he nodded. "Just taking a mental break from calls with my father."

"And how do you feel about that?" she asked. "Because I can give you privacy if you want to take it."

"No. That is his third call in twenty minutes," Jack told her.

"What if there's an emergency?"

Jack let out a frustrated sigh. "There's no emergency. Oh, he might think there's one, but it wouldn't be medical. It would be something to do with a listing or he's checking on the progress of the house. All of which can wait."

Rachel hesitated before adding, "You're sure he wouldn't call with an actual emergency?"

"I promise," he assured her. "He wouldn't even tell me if he had to go to the hospital until after the fact, and even then he'd blow it off. So, let's just enjoy the evening and not have my father join us as an absent third party."

She had to respect his wishes and believe he knew his father best. If he wanted a worry-free evening, then that was what Rachel would supply.

"So do you want to eat first or do you want your surprise?" she asked.

Even though she felt a little ridiculous with her gift, she still wanted to give it and see his reaction.

"A surprise?" Jack's brows rose as he took a step back. "You just put flowers in my house."

She didn't miss the way he said *his* house, but she wasn't about to call him on it. If he was getting used to being here, then so be it. And honestly, this area might be better for his mental well-being.

"The flowers were decoration," she corrected. "And because that space just called for it."

"So what's this surprise?"

"Oh, it's a necessity as well."

His warm laughter filled her tiny loft apartment and hit her right in her soul. She'd never felt more alive than when she was with Jack. Her adolescent crush had grown into something much larger and more complex than she could have ever dreamed. Part of her wanted to be completely open and honest about her feelings, but she didn't want to make things uncomfortable between them. There were too many working parts to their relationship, and throwing a wrench into any of that could jeopardize the solid bond they'd created.

"Well, you've intrigued me." He held out his hands. "Let's see this surprise."

Rachel spun around and went into her bedroom to retrieve the gift. Her cat shuffled somewhere beneath her bed, likely hiding from the visitor or curling up for a nap.

When she stepped back into the open space with her kitchen and living area, Jack was over by the Crock-Pot with the lid off.

"We can eat first," she told him. "Unless you're afraid of that lasagna."

He replaced the lid and turned to face her. "I've never

known how lasagna was made, but never would've guessed a Crock-Pot."

"Oh, it's normally in the oven in a large pan, but I wanted it to cook all day, so I tried this." She moved to the small round table that separated her living and kitchen area and set his present next to the small teacup of flowers she'd picked earlier today. "Here you go."

Jack's gaze shifted between the box and her, then back to the box.

"You wrapped it and everything?"

"Well, it is a gift."

Should she have just given it to him out of the shopping bag? That didn't seem proper at all. If she was going to do anything, she was going to do it right.

Jack closed the distance to the table and lifted the box. "It's heavy."

Rachel merely smiled as she waited for him to tear into it. She would've already had paper flying at this point if someone had presented her with a surprise.

He set the package back down and went to one of the folds on the end. Moving much slower than anyone should with a surprise, he lifted the flap.

"You know you didn't have to get me anything, right?" he asked, pulling the paper completely away.

"I'm well aware, but you needed this and I couldn't pass it up."

The paper fell to the floor and he stared down at the red box with a logo on the top that was so familiar to her but probably not to him. He glanced up once again with a crooked grin, like a kid on Christmas morning. Rachel didn't realize how special or exciting this would be, but she wanted to lock in this exact time and the look on his face. She hadn't seen him caught off guard or genuinely happy too often. So even if she felt silly about giving him something a touch extravagant, she would do it again in a heartbeat if that meant he was carefree for a short time.

"What's this?" he asked.

Yeah. He didn't know that brand or logo. Rachel merely shrugged.

"Lift the lid and find out."

He pulled the cardboard top off and shifted the tissue paper aside before stopping. Then he stared back up at her.

"You're kidding."

"Do you hate them?" she asked, now worried at his reaction.

"Hate them?" He chuckled as he pulled one dark brown cowboy boot from the box. "I never thought I'd say that I love these boots."

Relief replaced the worry, and she found herself smiling and taking a step toward him. "I'm so glad. When you stepped in the pile the other day, that pretty much convinced me you needed some farm-appropriate shoes. They'll be stiff at first, but once you wear them a bit, they'll be your favorite pair of shoes."

Jack pulled out one of the wooden chairs and took a seat. He immediately went to untying his sneakers and toeing them off. He set them aside and pulled out both boots, taking the stuffing out of each one and tossing it back into the box. Rachel waited while he slid into them.

When he came to his feet, she clasped her hands and did a little hop of excitement.

"Look at you," she declared. "You're practically a native now."

He walked around the table with an extra-exaggerated swagger that had her laughing even more.

"Is this how I do it?" he asked. "I feel like I need something plaid."

"We do not walk like that," she snorted.

"I did after I got off that horse the other day," he told her.

"Well, you look fine without anything plaid. And I hope you don't think I want to make you somebody that you aren't," she said. "I thought I'd buy them as a joke. Then that thought morphed into the realization that you might actually need them if you're going to come back from time to time. We don't want any more muck to tarnish that shine on your big boy shoes."

He stopped just before her and propped his hands on his hips. "Rachel, I would never in a million years think you were trying to make me into anyone else. Your gift came from the heart, and I can't tell you how much I love that you thought of me and were worried for my other shoes."

His smile and teasing, and his compliment, had those giddy emotions swirling through once again. But had they ever stopped? Since she'd ridden over to the Circle H that first day, she'd been in a constant state of awareness and attraction.

"You don't have to wear them right now," she told him. "You can put your sneakers back on."

He snapped his head back in mock shock. "Are you kidding me? I don't know the last time I received a gift. I'm wearing these all night."

"You don't know when you received a gift last?" she repeated, her chest tightening just a bit. "Christmas? A birthday?"

"I'm too old for birthday gifts, and for Christmas my father typically puts extra money in my bonus for the end of the year commission," he said matter-of-factly. "So, if that counts."

"No, it doesn't."

And she was truly starting to see why Jack seemed so happy here. No expectations, no one bribing him or trying to use him for gains. She might not know Jack's father, but she didn't like the man. Which just proved to her she needed to pray harder for him. Anyone who was that absorbed with the ways of the world and hungry for more power needed guidance and God. It wasn't her place to judge, but it was her place to look out for her friend.

"How about we eat?" she suggested. "You sit and I'll get everything ready."

"I can help," he offered. "Let me mosey on over and I can get our drinks."

Rachel held up a hand to stop him. "You can't just throw on the boots and turn instant cowboy with a swagger and the lingo. You've got to ease into this lifestyle."

He hooked his thumbs through his belt loops and tipped his head. "I've been here a couple weeks now. I think my next step is a big hat and a horse."

She dropped her hand and snickered as she made her way to the open shelving above her counters. She grabbed two yellow plates and set them next to the Crock-Pot.

"If you were staying, I'd help you shop for the perfect horse." She lifted the lid and scooped out a healthy portion for Jack. "But you can borrow Champ on your visits."

"I'd like that."

She wasn't sure what the future held for either of them and the farm, but for tonight, she was going to enjoy their time together and not worry about the outside world or tomorrow. God had a plan, and this was where her faith and her trust had to take over.

Chapter Thirteen

Jack figured since several rooms in the farmhouse had turned into a construction zone, he might as well decide what to do about all of his grandfather's things in the main barn. He unlocked the side door and slid the key back into his pocket. He reached in and felt for the light switch and flicked it on.

The old space had that musty smell from being closed up for a while, and Jack hadn't made it down here since his return. He'd been busy with more important things and figured when he sold the place, nobody would care if the barn looked all glitzy. The house was a different story, though, so he'd kept his focus on that.

His booted heels clicked on the concrete floor, echoing throughout the empty space.

Jack merely stood and took in his surroundings. It had been years since he'd been in this area and he needed a moment. The memories came rolling in one by one. The first time he learned how to groom a horse, the first time his grandfather taught him how to clean a stall. Grunt work was all part of the life of a rancher. His grandfather always told him you had to put in the work to reap the rewards.

So many life lessons learned on this farm and here in this barn. Jack wasn't sure he fully appreciated the moments at the time, but looking back, he loved all that his grandfather had instilled in him.

He also couldn't help but wonder why his father was so anti–farm life and shunned anything to do with the Circle H. Clearly something happened between his dad and grandfather, something that had driven a wedge between them. Thankfully, Jack hadn't been pushed out of his grandfather's life.

Jack headed toward the office area and turned the knob. The moment the old wooden door swung open, Jack was faced with another old desk, where his grandfather would pour hours into his work. Jack was taking the one from the house and knew he couldn't take this desk, too. There would be no need for two desks, so he'd probably leave this one in the barn for the new owner.

An instant image of Rachel sitting in that rickety old chair gave him pause. Everywhere he looked at the Circle H, he could see her making her mark and continuing what his grandfather had started.

And for the first time, Jack wondered what his grandfather would want done here. Jack knew money never mattered to his grandfather, not the way Jack's father coveted it. Traditions and morals and his faith were the staples in George's life up until he passed.

Had Jack inherited all of this because his grandfather wanted him here? Did he want Jack to carry on the Circle H into a new generation? How could Jack decide between his father and his grandfather's wishes?

Or maybe he was supposed to do what felt right to *him* and no one else. He could really use some of that faith Rachel relied on. He needed guidance because he was so utterly confused.

Swallowing the lump of remorse and guilt in his throat,

Jack moved around the desk to see if there were any personal items left. He had no clue what his grandfather kept in here. All of the actual business paperwork was up in the study at the farmhouse.

Jack rolled the old chair aside and started with the top middle drawer. A few random pens, some blank sticky notes, a few unwrapped pieces of hard candy that made Jack chuckle. Cherry, of course. Jack recalled finding those little red candies all over the house. His grandfather always said being outside so much made his throat dry. Jack remembered sneaking pieces for himself until he found an entire bag on his nightstand one morning and knew his grandfather had been onto him. He'd never said a word and Jack only told him thanks.

He closed that drawer and reached for the top right and gave a tug. A variety of worn notebooks and journals were all that was in this drawer. Jack reached in, pulled out one of the books and flipped it open. He stilled at the familiar sight of his grandfather's elegant cursive writing. On closer inspection, Jack realized this wasn't a business journal but a personal one. Why would he have such a thing out here?

Jack felt for the chair he'd shoved away moments ago and sank onto the creaky leather. He flipped back to the first page to start at the beginning. This journal was dated about twenty years ago. Even though the pages weren't too worn or torn, he still turned them carefully. He had a feeling he'd be getting nothing else done today except reading these journals. Perhaps that was what his grandfather had been doing at this desk for hours. He'd been pouring his thoughts out onto paper.

Part of Jack felt like he was violating his grandfather's

privacy, but the other part wanted to feel closer to the man who'd had a small part in shaping the person he was today.

Spring is the most exciting time. All the babies are born and bringing new life to the farm. This year I will try to hire a couple boys from the local high school to help around the place. Jack will be here in just over a month, and I can't wait to see him. He's the brightest point in the year for me. The house gets lonely without Bonnie here. Jack really fills a void, and he's growing into such a nice young man. I can't wait to see how much he's changed and what he remembers from last summer.

The words blurred and Jack realized his emotions were getting the best of him. He hadn't cried since coming back. He'd been in work mode and caught up with Rachel, and maybe there was a part of him that simply didn't want to face that hurt.

Jack turned the page and blinked away the unshed tears. He wanted to concentrate on each word and knew without a doubt he'd find a special place for these journals. Nobody needed to know about these, and honestly, Jack didn't feel like his father deserved to know. Likely he wouldn't care anyway, but Jack planned on keeping this precious secret to himself.

"I think the rosemary bundles need to go on top of the napkin on the plate," Sarah Spencer stated as she came up to the long dining table in the barn.

Violet rearranged the place setting and stepped back. "Like that?"

"That definitely looks better," Rachel agreed from the other side of the table. "I like the look we're doing on this dinner."

She set a tall bundle of pampas grass in the middle of

the table and adjusted a few of the pieces to balance out the simple arrangement. Tonight they were having another farm-to-table event, but this one was for a bridal shower. A small, modest gathering with only about twenty-five people, but no matter the size of the party, the Spencer ladies always wanted each guest to feel like they were special.

"I do, too," Erin agreed as she slid the white slipcovers over the chairs at the opposite end of the table. "The bride requested neutrals and elegant, so I think we did pretty good."

Rachel loved the gift table with a nice photo of the couple and a large prop initial *B* for the last name they would share. The letter had been made of wood and brought from the bride to use with the decor. The piece had been hollowed out and Erin had placed gorgeous cream and white flowers stuffed neatly with various pops of greenery.

Rachel turned from the table where her mom and sisters were working and went to the food tables. She could go ahead and get the cupcake stand set up and the macarons displayed. The bride had also sent over her great-grandmother's white serving platter, which she wanted incorporated, and Rachel thought the pistachio macarons would look perfect on that piece.

She couldn't wait to have her own bridal shower one day. Maybe she'd do one just like this, here on the farm. She definitely wanted small and intimate. Just a cozy gathering for her family and closest friends.

"Need help?"

Rachel turned as Jenn came up to her side.

"If you want to do the cupcake stand, I can get the macarons ready," she told her. "The boxes are in the kitchen."

They'd transformed this barn space into something amaz-

ing over the past several months. The town had really embraced the farm-to-table idea. What had started as a prayer
to help save the farm quickly turned into something bigger
than they ever could have imagined.

Rachel hoped this venture would last generations and
continue to bring families and the community together.
She yearned for a family of her own to pass her own traditions down to.

"You seem lost in thought," Jenn stated. "Everything
okay?"

Rachel tucked a wayward strand that had slid from her
braid back behind her ear as she turned toward her sister. "I'm fine. I just love all of this. Your wedding coming
up, this bridal shower. It just leaves me feeling so happy
and hopeful."

Jenn reached for her hand and gripped in that tender way
she had. "Rach, you will find the right one at the right time.
You have so much to offer, and just because Tyler didn't
have the same vision doesn't mean he was your only chance
at love. He was a great guy, just not the right fit for you."

"I know," Rachel agreed. "He wouldn't have been happy
here and I wouldn't have been happy in a big city where
he wanted to be. I think I just worry because I'm the oldest sister and what if I get too old?"

Jenn let out a soft laugh. "Too old for what? Love has
no expiration."

"For children," Rachel admitted. "What if I get too old
to have my own family?"

Their mother and other two sisters were chattering
about which drink glasses to use while Rachel was having a slight pity moment.

"What if you meet someone with a child already?" Jenn
countered. "I met Luke and his sweet niece and we will

raise her together. I'm not sure if we'll have children of our own or if Paisley will be it, but I know that God's plan worked out perfectly after my husband passed. I never thought I'd be happy again, let alone find love."

"You don't know how glad I am that you're back home." Rachel pulled her sister into a hug, because they still had a three-year gap to make up for. "You're right where you belong, and Luke and Paisley are lucky to have you."

Jenn eased back and nodded. "We're lucky to have found each other. And may I say something and not be offensive?"

Rachel pulled back slightly but held on to her sister's hand. "That's a loaded question."

"I just can't help but wonder if Jack came into town at this precise time for a reason," Jenn stated. "I mean, he wasn't here for George's funeral, but he's here now and he seems to be quite attached to you."

Attached? That wasn't quite the word Rachel would use.

"First, I'm not offended," Rachel started. "Second, he's here now because he has to sell the home and get back to his life in San Francisco. His father tasked him with the Rosewood Valley properties."

"All in God's timing," Jenn repeated.

Rachel's heart fluttered. If Jack even had an inkling of an idea of staying, she would embrace every part of that. She could see him here in ways she could never see Tyler. Jack seemed happier and more relaxed here, and frustrated when he discussed his life back home. Was he in a hurry to get back to the stress and day-to-day rush?

No matter what he was feeling, Rachel couldn't help but have a sliver of panic with how fast her emotions had grown toward him. Try as she might, she couldn't seem to get control over how she felt toward her childhood crush. But she needed to slow down; she needed restraint over her thoughts and the direction of her heart. She could only pray she didn't get hurt again, but she was human and couldn't help who she was drawn to.

"Well, right now we're going to concentrate on this bride," Rachel told Jenn. "And in a couple weeks, we're going to concentrate on you. My time will come. I'm going to believe that. Until then, I will celebrate you."

Jenn gave her one final hug before going to the kitchen to retrieve the boxes. Rachel blew out a breath and wished she had the courage to just tell Jack how she felt. But if she did and he left like he said he would, she'd look and feel like a fool again. Risking her heart wasn't something she was ready for. So until or unless Jack indicated he wanted to remain in Rosewood Valley, she'd have to keep those thoughts and feelings locked deep inside her heart.

Chapter Fourteen

Jack felt ridiculous now that he was here, but he'd already pulled into the drive and been spotted by Will Spencer, so there was no backing out now.

He put his car in Park and killed the engine. He'd spent all night reading his grandfather's journals, and this morning he wanted to talk to the one person who might have been the closest to the man he'd lost. Will was not only a fellow farmer but a close neighbor. No doubt they'd shared stories and confided in each other over the years. After seeing Will's name multiple times in the journals, Jack realized those two had to have had a special bond.

"Mornin'," Will called through the barn opening.

Jack waved. "Morning. Is this a bad time for a visit?"

"Rachel is in the house with Sarah, if you're looking for her."

Jack wouldn't turn down a moment to see Rachel, but that would have to wait.

"I'm actually here to see you."

Will gripped his red suspenders and nodded. "This is a good time, then. You want a cup of coffee? We can head to the house."

"No, no. I'm good." Jack really didn't know what to say now that he was here, but he wanted another connection to his grandfather. "I know we don't really know each other—"

"I feel I know you pretty well," Will stated. "George spoke about you pretty often, and when you were young and visited, I recall a few times when you all came over."

Yeah, Jack remembered coming to the barns here and discussing livestock.

"I just wanted to talk to you about the Circle H and the direction I'm going." Jack shrugged and looped his thumbs through his belt loops. "I plan on selling as soon as the minor renovations are complete. I guess I'm feeling a little guilty about it, and I just want to make sure the right person gets it and I make my grandfather proud. I figure you knew him best from anyone in town, other than Walt at the store."

"Your grandfather and I were pretty close over the years," Will agreed. "I valued our friendship and continue to mourn the loss."

George Hart had made his presence known in Rosewood Valley—that much was certain. Jack was proud to be the grandson of a man who had been so highly thought of.

"I also think he'd want you to do what is best for not only the farm, but for you as well," Will added. "He loved you and was so proud of you. He wouldn't want anything to be a burden."

No, he wouldn't. Jack could definitely agree with that. His grandfather wanted others to be happy, and he constantly put himself second...much like Rachel. Maybe that was why he felt such a connection to her. That giving spirit inside her and the compassion and bright light she projected made him feel so at home in ways he never would have imagined.

"The property isn't a burden," Jack replied, crossing his arms over his chest. "I just don't have a need for it and I do need to sell it for top dollar."

"Money never mattered to George."

"No, just my father," Jack muttered. "It's important that I get the most I can from the land and farmhouse for reasons I can't get into."

Or didn't want to get into.

Maybe if Jack was honest, money had mattered more to him at one time, too. He couldn't deny the thrill of success and accolades from associates. But since coming to this small, humble town, Jack realized maybe money didn't always have to be the end goal.

"Rachel has wanted that farm for years," Will stated. "Her dream has been to join the two properties and ultimately pass down her part to her family, because this land will always be Spencer land."

"She told me she wanted the property," Jack confirmed. "I just can't lease or rent it to sell. It's a long story."

Will nodded and blew out a long sigh. "If I could buy that place for her, I would in a heartbeat. That girl does everything for everyone else. Sold her own home not long ago to help her mother and me around here. She puts those around her first and herself last."

"I've noticed that."

Will's bushy silver brows drew in. "You and Rachel have gotten close since you've come to town."

Jack didn't want to make anyone believe they had anything beyond a friendship. He wasn't staying, and no matter what feelings he might have developed, it wouldn't be fair to her to express them.

"She's become a great friend," Jack replied honestly. "She's been a huge help with ideas on the house, and I know nothing about a feed store, so she's been putting in a few hours there helping as well."

"That girl." Will shook his head. "She told me she was working some for extra money. She'd do anything to get her own place. She's wearing herself too thin, if you ask me."

Jack agreed, but he hadn't come here to get Will worked up over Rachel's hectic schedule. He truly wanted advice. Maybe he wanted fatherly advice he couldn't get from his own dad.

Jack glanced around the barn and noticed it was smaller than the one his grandfather had used the most. Will's had four stalls where the Circle H had eight. Both properties had more than one barn for livestock, but his grandfather's sat empty now, just waiting on a new owner to bring in their chosen stock. George had sold his animals a couple of years ago as his health started to make the hard work more difficult. He'd kept his focus on the store, which was easier to maintain, especially with Walt's help.

"I respect you guys so much," Jack stated as he moved toward the first stall, where Champ stood. "The hard work ranchers and farmers put in typically goes unnoticed."

"That's not why we do the work." Will turned to face Jack and adjusted his worn cowboy hat. "We love the tradition and the land. We love knowing we are providing for our families and instilling morals and work ethic that will be passed down."

Jack reached through the wrought iron bars and slid his hand over Champ's velvety nose. Tradition and tight family bonds seemed to be the theme through Rosewood Valley. Jack couldn't help but wonder if his grandfather had been depressed or upset knowing Jack's father would never take over the land. Had George Hart wanted the

Circle H to go to his only child and a new generation to grow with the times while still keeping those values and traditions?

"I just wish I knew the right thing to do for everyone, including my grandfather." Jack dropped his hand and glanced back at Will. "Believe me, if I could gift this to Rachel, I would. There's just more to it than that. I know she'd take care of the land like my grandfather would've wanted. And I know there's nobody better fitting to work it and run it."

"You don't have to explain yourself to me," Will chimed in. "You can't just give away something like that, and I know you are a city businessman. You all think differently than rural folks do and that's okay. The good Lord made us all different or this would be a boring world."

Jack chuckled at the accurate statement. "I guess if we were all working from an office, nothing much would get done by way of agriculture."

Will nodded. "You got that right. But I couldn't work in an office, so there's a reason God made all the variety. We all have our strengths."

"I'm wondering if I even know mine anymore," Jack muttered.

"What's that nonsense talk?" Will grumbled. "George followed your career and would brag how well you were doing."

"Did he?" Jack asked. "Once I graduated college and tried making a name for myself, all I could focus on was work. Being self-employed is difficult, as you know. If I don't work, I'm not getting paid. I guess I got so wrapped up in trying to lay a firm foundation, I didn't get back for those visits like I'd always done."

"I won't lie," Will added. "George sure did miss seeing you, but he knew you'd grow up and get a life of your own."

A life of his own? Jack wondered lately who he'd been living that life for. He'd always wanted to make his father proud, but the constant jumping through hoops was starting to wear on him. Maybe once this farmhouse was complete and on the market, his father would see the hard work he'd put into his childhood home. Jack hoped, anyway.

"If you don't mind my saying, you look torn or worried."

Will's observation had Jack blinking back to the moment and stepping out of his thoughts.

"I'm both," he answered. Why lie? "I have no need for a farm, but it's difficult to say goodbye to a place that holds so many core childhood memories."

"I've never had to let go of something I loved before," Will admitted. "I don't know what I'd do without the Four Sisters, and I hope I never have to find that out."

Jack wasn't sure what to say. He didn't have any more clarity than when he'd walked in here.

"I wasn't sure what would happen to the farm once your grandfather passed," Will went on. "But I'm not surprised you were the beneficiary. George loved the summers you spent here."

As if Jack needed another dose of guilt. But he couldn't deny that those summers had been some of the best moments and fondest memories of his entire life.

"What happens if you don't sell right away?" Will proposed. "I'm not sure of your circumstances, but if you prayed over your situation and waited for God's guidance, that might help."

Pray over this? Jack didn't recall praying over any business dealings he'd done in the past. Maybe he should give that a try. It wasn't that he didn't believe in God. He knew all the good things in his life came from above. He'd just got so busy climbing that invisible corporate ladder that he'd put his faith on the back burner.

Being back here, though, reminded him of how important faith was.

"I'm not sure if I helped your decision," Will went on. "I know George wouldn't want you to be torn up over this, but he definitely would want his farm going to someone who would love and appreciate it like he did."

Jack nodded and attempted a grin. "I appreciate your advice. I will pray on my decision. I guess I just needed someone to guide me in that direction."

"I'm here anytime you need to talk," Will offered. "And Rachel is a great listener, too."

"She's pretty amazing," Jack agreed. "I'll let you get back to work."

Jack started to walk out of the barn when Will called his name. Jack turned to look over his shoulder.

"I know you both say you're just friends," Will started, gripping those red straps once again. "But you're both so quick to remind people of that, it makes me wonder if you're keeping those real feelings buried. Maybe add that to your prayer list as well."

Jack couldn't help but bite the inside of his cheek as he tried to suppress the grin. Will was of the generation of the wise and observant.

"I need to add quite a bit to my prayer list," Jack replied, then turned on his new boots and headed back to his car.

He pulled his sunglasses down to shield the sun, and movement from the kitchen window caught his eye. Rachel stood on the other side, waving with a wide smile spread across her face.

Yes. He had quite a bit to pray about.

* * *

"I cannot believe this."

Rachel glanced up from her laptop as Violet burst through her loft door. Rach never expected family to knock, and she left her door unlocked unless she was asleep.

Since she'd just submitted an online quiz, she shut her laptop to focus on her sister and the paper she was waving in the air.

"Calm down," Rachel said as she came to her feet and set her laptop on the coffee table. "What happened?"

"A fine from the new sheriff." Vi shut the door behind her and stepped forward, thrusting the paper in Rachel's direction. "I mean, this is how he wants to introduce himself?"

Rachel took the paper and ran her gaze across it to see what the fine could be about.

"It's just a parking violation," Rachel explained. "So park somewhere else."

Vi scoffed and snatched the paper back, crumpling it in her hand. "I've been parking in the same spot for eight years. The old sheriff didn't have a problem with it, nor has any other law enforcement officer in Rosewood Valley."

Rachel slid the band from the bottom of her braid and loosened the strands. "Did this come in the mail?"

"No. He hand-delivered it to my office staff," she explained. "Didn't even wait to hand it straight to me or introduce himself."

Rachel tried not to laugh at how worked up Violet seemed to be. Out of all the sisters, Vi had very little patience with people, but all the patience in the world for her pet clients.

"I've been so busy with everything, I forgot I heard

we were getting a new sheriff," Rachel stated. "Do you know his name?"

Violet carefully unwrapped the wad in her hand and glanced at the page. "Dax Adams. Dax. What kind of name is that?"

Rachel couldn't help the snicker that escaped her, but then she remembered her morals. "Be nice. He's new and just doing his job."

"I'm sure there's other things he can be doing other than harassing a local business owner."

Rachel tucked her hair behind her ears and held her sister's frustrated gaze. "I wouldn't call this harassing," she replied. "He didn't even speak to you."

Violet's brows drew in as she shoved the paper back into the pocket of her gray scrub top. "Why are you coming to his defense?" she asked, crossing her arms. "I thought you had a thing for Jack."

Rachel jerked. "I most certainly do not."

Vi rolled her eyes. "Rach, it's me. I know you better than anyone, except Erin and Jenn. None of us can lie to each other. You know that."

Rachel shrugged and turned to sink back onto her vacated nook in the corner of her small sectional sofa. "So what if I like him? That means nothing."

Violet remained unmoving, but that intense stare locked in on Rachel.

"What?" she asked. "I admitted I like him. What more do you want from me?"

"Did you tell him?"

"Why would I do that?" Rachel retorted. "He's a great guy and he's made it clear this isn't the life for him. I wouldn't tell him something to make him feel guilty or pity me."

Violet moved around the end table and took a seat on the sofa. "Did you ever think he might have grown feelings for you, too? That maybe it's not fair to either of you to keep how you feel a secret?"

Rachel glanced away and stared at her closed laptop… which held another secret she'd been keeping. Maybe she didn't want to be rejected again if she told Jack how she felt. That was a very realistic outcome and one she never wanted to face again.

"He's not Tyler," Violet murmured, taking Rachel's hand in hers. "I think you need to give him a chance. Jack could be keeping his feelings bottled up as well."

Rachel wasn't naive. She knew Jack liked her, but did he *like* her? Should she tell him how she felt and just take a chance? Did she want to risk her heart again?

"Let me ask you this," Violet added. "If he leaves town, will you regret not saying anything? You have to think about that."

Rachel's heart swelled and she pulled in a deep breath. Yes. She would have regrets if Jack left and her feelings remained locked tight inside. Maybe being completely open and up-front was just how she'd have to handle this and then leave the decision to him. She wouldn't beg and she wouldn't want him to compromise who he was. That wouldn't be any type of relationship.

So now the question was, when would she tell him?

Chapter Fifteen

The progress on the house was coming along faster than he'd thought, but Jack wanted to step away. He hadn't seen Rachel since the day before yesterday. They'd texted a few times, but nothing of real substance. He was torn and confused and really just needed to see her. Something about Rachel gave him peace and clarity when his world seemed to be complicated lately.

Before he'd arrived in Rosewood Valley, Jack figured he'd get into town, have a few rooms painted and staged, put the house up for sale and leave with a record number sale. But life had a weird way of showing who was in charge…and it wasn't Jack.

He'd taken the past day and a half and really tried praying like Will suggested. And although Jack was still confused, he felt better knowing he had God on his side. But he still wished he knew the right answer and where to go from here.

He mounted the steps to Rachel's loft and tapped on the door.

The door burst open. "Are you still upset about the violation?"

Rachel stopped abruptly. "Oh, sorry." She laughed. "I thought you were Vi again. She just left a bit ago."

"Just me," he stated, holding his hands out. "Bad time?"

He glanced at her long, flowy dress and her hair around her shoulders. This wasn't the Rachel who worked around the farm or feed store or the one who helped him brainstorm renovations. This Rachel looked quite different and equally as stunning.

"Not at all," she told him. "Come on in. I was just trying on my bridesmaid's dress again since it got hemmed. I'm trying to decide on the right shoes."

He stepped inside and closed the door behind him. "Well, you look beautiful."

Her smile spread across her face, and just that simple gesture calmed him and soothed his soul. How did she do that? He'd never met a woman who managed to have such a hold over his emotions and she likely didn't have a clue.

"Thank you," she replied. "Are you hungry? I haven't made dinner yet, but I can change and whip something up."

"I didn't come by so you'd feed me again," he explained. "I came by because I missed you."

Her mouth dropped open. "Missed me? I don't think anyone has ever missed me before. Or if they have, they've never told me."

That was a shame. The gap in their nearly two days apart had left him a little unsettled...so what would that lead to once he went back home and didn't see her for what would likely be months?

"Let me get changed and then we can talk." She started to turn toward her bedroom, then tossed a glance over her shoulder. "And I missed you, too."

As she walked away, a cat darted from beneath the sofa and straight into her room just before Rachel closed the door.

He raked a hand down his face and glanced around the

small living area. Granted, she lived alone, but his penthouse apartment had to be five times this size. Yet the more he looked, the more he realized she had everything anyone needed. Fully stocked kitchen, table and chairs for dining, a small sectional sofa, coffee table, television. Her bedroom had a bath off it and she was happy and content. Yes, she wanted her own farm, but Jack knew in his heart she didn't care about the size of the house she lived in. All Rachel wanted was land for animals and to raise a family. Her dreams and wishes would seem simple to most people, but they were everything to her.

Moments later she came back out with her jeans, a plain long-sleeve red T-shirt and her hair back in that signature braid. Her pitcher necklace hung around her neck, and he loved how she and her sisters and mother shared that symbol of giving and love. What would that be like to have such a wholesome foundation? To have love and unconditional support from so many family members?

"Hey. You okay?"

Rachel's concerning tone pulled him back to the present. But instead of nodding and playing everything off, he shook his head.

"Not really," he admitted.

Instantly she crossed the space between them and took his hand in hers as those green eyes came up to meet his. "Talk to me."

Jack reached for her other hand so he securely held on to both. "I don't even know what to say except I'm just glad I met you. You've given me some reprieve from the stress of the house and the store. I know I can talk to you about anything and trust it stays between us."

"Of course."

That sweet grin of hers hit him straight in the heart

once again. How could life be so complicated? How could he meet and fall for a woman who led a completely opposite life and lived hundreds of miles from him? Was that how God's plans worked? He presented His plan and you had to figure out how to make a go of it?

"You look more stressed now than I've ever seen you," Rachel stated. "Do you want to have a seat?"

She led him to the sofa, and the moment he eased down, she sat right next to him, still holding on to one of his hands.

"Did you find out something with the store?" she asked.

"Not yet."

"Is there a hiccup with the renovations?"

He shook his head. "We're actually ahead of schedule."

"Something with your dad?"

Something with you.

"No. I actually haven't talked to him in a few days. I texted and told him I was busy and I'd get back to him once I got the house on the market."

"Well, if it makes you feel better, you got an A on that essay you helped me with."

A sliver of relief slid through him, and he hadn't even realized how much he cared about her grade until now.

"That's good to hear," he replied.

"We make a pretty great team with several things," she informed him. "Are you sure I can't fix us something for dinner?"

"I don't expect that."

"So you already told me," she reminded him. "But I'm getting hungry and you're here and could clearly use some company and comfort food."

Yes, but he could use clarity more than anything. And

being closed up with Rachel only made him more confused about what he wanted.

"Isn't there a good place in town to grab home-cooked food?" he asked.

"There are a couple of places." She narrowed her eyes and tipped her head. "Are you asking me on a date or are you afraid of my cooking?"

"I'm not afraid of your cooking."

She blinked and her hold on his hand relaxed. "Oh, um…yes. We could do that. I need to put on something else and—"

"You look beautiful just like always," he interjected. "You never have to get made up to do anything with me. I like you just the way you are."

There. He'd placed those delicate, loaded words right between them. She could interpret that as friends or more. He wanted to gauge her reaction before he could figure out his next move.

But again, he needed to pray on it. No matter what he wanted to do, he had to go to prayer to make sure that was what God wanted him to do.

"Can I at least grab my boots?" she asked with a chuckle.

"You can do that, but you don't need anything else."

When he came to his feet, he took her hand and pulled her up with him. He didn't know what he was thinking or how to label his emotions, but leaning in and placing his lips against hers just seemed right. With their hands trapped between their bodies, Rachel relaxed against him and sank into the kiss. Jack hadn't been sure of her feelings, but that one simple gesture said more than any words ever could.

Now he had even more to think about. Rachel had feelings for him just like he did for her.

When he eased back, her lids fluttered open, revealing those expressive green eyes that he'd come to love.

Love?

Yes. Love. He was falling for her, and he wasn't sure when that had happened. Had the transition been slow or had he fallen the moment she'd professed her adolescent crush that first day she rode up on her horse?

"I hope I didn't overstep," he murmured.

"I'm wondering what took you so long to make that move," she threw back with a slight grin.

His heart swelled, and he couldn't dwell on everything that could go wrong if they pursued a romance. He didn't want to dwell on negativity. For his time in town and with Rachel, he wanted his sole focus to be on her. Maybe through his new prayer habits and spending more time with her, his answer would become clearer.

Rachel wasn't sure what was happening, but she also wasn't going to question it.

She and Jack had grabbed dinner at Fork 'n' Finger. She'd had the chicken and noodles and Jack had gone with the steak and fried potatoes with green beans. Definitely some comfort food, and Rachel didn't know if it was the tender kiss or the hot meal that had perked up his spirits.

And somehow they'd ended up in the den sanding those built-ins.

"I have no clue what I'm doing," Jack muttered. "I always hire for this work to get done."

Rachel laughed and dropped her sandpaper to the drop cloth beneath her feet. She moved to the other end of the wall where Jack worked on his section. She glanced at what he'd done and nodded.

"Look at you for excelling at yet another thing outside

your comfort zone," she joked. "First saddling a horse, then the boots and now sanding. Better watch yourself. You'll want to keep this place for yourself and you'll be buying a horse next."

Jack shook his head. "I don't see me buying a horse anytime soon."

"Sanding and staining is grunt work." Rachel ran her fingertips over the lighter area that he'd already smoothed out. "It's time-consuming, but so worth it in the end when you sit back and see your finished product."

"You've done this before, I take it?"

She turned her attention to him, noting again how those dark eyes could draw her in and mesmerize her. The invisible pull between them only seemed to grow stronger, and the thought of him leaving made her heart ache.

"I did the table in my living room, and I helped my mom with the old bookshelves she put in my bedroom when I was a teen."

Jack reached up and swiped the pad of his thumb across her cheek. "You had some sanding dust," he explained as he dropped his hand to his side.

That brief, innocent touch had a whole host of new emotions running through her. She was falling for him and there was absolutely no denying this fact anymore. She'd promised herself she'd try to keep her feelings in check, that she'd put up an emotional barrier, but her human tendencies had taken over and now she had herself a predicament.

"Thanks," she murmured. "You're doing a great job. It's just not going to be done tonight or even tomorrow. But we'll get it."

A smile flirted around his mouth. "I like the fact you're helping me. With everything, really. The farm, the store."

"Maybe we make a good team," she suggested, forcing a smile when her heart was beating much too fast and her stomach was in knots.

"I'm starting to think we do."

His gaze dropped to her mouth, but the chime that echoed through the house pulled her attention away from the tender moment.

"Was that the driveway alarm?" she asked.

Jack nodded. "I'm not expecting anyone."

He started from the room and Rachel pulled in a deep breath as she followed him. She had no clue who this unexpected guest was, but she should probably be thankful because she had a feeling he'd been about to kiss her and all that would do was make her fall even more.

As they reached the foyer, Jack glanced out the sidelight to the drive. The porch lights and the glow from the barn lights lit up the space and Jack came to a halt and gasped.

"Is that a worker?" she asked. "It's kind of late for them, isn't it?"

"That's not a worker."

Jack's words had a whole new tone—one she didn't recognize.

"That's my father."

Chapter Sixteen

❧

Jack wished he was home alone. Rachel shouldn't have to be here to see his father, whom Jack had certainly not been expecting. He hadn't told Jack he was coming, and Jack imagined this little surprise was exactly how Logan Hart wanted it to be. To catch Jack off guard and check in on progress. Great. Just great.

"I can't wait to meet him," Rachel stated as she started toward the front door.

That was such a Rachel comment and gesture. Always looking for the positive, but Jack wasn't feeling so warm and fuzzy. What had gone from a beautiful evening could very well go south quickly.

"I can run you home," Jack offered.

"No. I'd like to meet your father. I loved George and I…I adore you. It's only fitting I meet your dad, too. What's his name?"

"Logan."

Jack reached around her to unlock the door but didn't miss that she'd said she adored him. With all the turmoil rolling around inside him over his decisions and now facing his father, he couldn't quite delve into what she'd just revealed. And maybe a slipup was all that was. But he'd have to figure that out later.

Rachel was already stepping onto the porch, ready to

greet his father. Jack pulled in a deep breath as he moved ahead of her. With a gentle grasp, he took her elbow. He didn't know if he was wanting her to stop here and wait on his father to come up or if he just needed to cling to her for a little emotional support. Either way, he was glad she was here. Even if he wasn't quite comfortable with his father meeting her, Jack had come to rely on Rachel for much more than he could've ever imagined.

"Just keep in mind, he's nothing like people around here," Jack warned. "He's harder, no-nonsense."

Rachel turned and patted his cheek. "I can handle myself."

Looking into those wide eyes, Jack truly believed she could, but he still wanted to wrap her up and protect her and give her all the good in life she deserved. He only hoped his father wasn't too harsh and only talking business.

"Dad," Jack greeted him. "I wish I'd known you were coming. I would've been here or made sure a room was ready for you."

"When you weren't taking my calls and only resorting to texts, I assumed something was wrong, so I had to come out and see for myself."

"Everything is going according to plan," Jack replied, leaving out the part about the sidetrack of his plan with Rachel. He certainly hadn't expected to find someone to throw his entire world for a proverbial loop.

"I thought this place would be on the market by now," his father practically grumbled as he stepped up onto the porch.

Jack took a step forward, but Rachel stepped in front of him. "Hi. I'm Rachel Spencer. I live on the farm next door. Your father was an amazing man and we definitely miss him."

Jack waited, holding his breath, hoping his father would turn on some sort of manners.

"Yes, he was an amazing man," his dad agreed, his eyes darting between them. "Are you and my son dating?"

"Dad."

"No."

Jack and Rachel spoke at the same time, but Jack stepped up next to Rachel.

"Even if I was dating anyone, that has nothing to do with the house," Jack started. "Rachel has been helping me with renovation ideas, and she's extremely knowledgeable with the town, which will help with finding the right buyer."

Rachel tensed beside him. Jack shouldn't be surprised at his father's business-only approach. The only reason his dad had asked about dating was because he wouldn't want it to interfere with the progress and sale. Jack didn't have to ask; he knew Logan Hart better than anyone.

"Why don't we go inside so you can see some of the progress and Jack's ideas?" Rachel suggested.

While Jack appreciated her big heart and peacemaker ways, he didn't want her in the middle of this. But they all three moved into the foyer and Jack closed the door behind them.

His father glanced around, down the hallway, trying to see toward the kitchen, and then to the right toward the family room.

"How soon will the farm get listed?" he asked. "Have you scheduled an open house for after the renovations or anything yet?"

"I don't think an open house will be necessary," Jack replied. "Rosewood Valley is pretty laid-back and everyone around here already knows this farm well and what a prime piece of real estate it is."

His father unbuttoned his suit jacket and sighed as he rested his hands on his hips. "You know how this business works, son. There's a method to flipping and selling. I hope you're not getting caught up in sentimental memories and delaying listing this place."

Jack ground his teeth and pulled in a deep breath as he sent up a prayer for patience. He'd dealt with this type of behavior from his father his entire life, but it wasn't until coming to Rosewood Valley and seeing the dynamics of the Spencers and dealing with a home that housed so many precious moments that Jack came to the realization that there was more than the almighty dollar. Yes, he still wanted that promotion, but all of this had become a learning experience. Money wasn't everything and he could still get that office he'd worked so hard for.

"I'm well aware how the business works," Jack replied. "Which is why I also know my market in this area, and wasting money on an open house is not what I plan on doing. The home will be on the market in less than three weeks. I'll have it sold in less than a week once it is listed."

"Brian recently sold a commercial building." His father rattled off a staggering number. "I'm sure you know that's a company record."

"Good for him."

Jack truly was happy for Brian. They were all on the same team for Hart Realty. Jack still felt like he deserved the promotion over a man who had only been with the company for three years.

"I need this project wrapped up and you back in the office," his father went on. "We have bigger listings and the new location needs someone in it full-time."

"Isn't Brian there?"

"He's going back and forth. If you would have answered

my calls over the past few days, I could have saved this trip." His father glanced around and then back to Rachel. "But I'm glad I came, because I'm starting to see what the holdup is."

Jack opened his mouth, but Rachel beat him to it.

"Mr. Hart, Jack has been extremely hands-on with this home and the feed store. He's been taking the time to get to know the people of the town just like your father did. While the contractors are here, Jack is planning the best way to market this land to not only get the best price, but also to make sure your father's legacy is still honored. It's quite a feat for such a short time."

Of course Rachel would continue to come to his defense. And while he shouldn't be surprised that she'd hyped him up and mentioned putting the house on the market, he still was because she'd not once mentioned herself or that she wanted the land yet couldn't afford it.

She didn't have to say a word, yet she did on his behalf.

When his father continued to stare at Rachel like she was insane for coming to his defense, Jack wanted her out of here.

"I'm going to run her home and then I'll be back," Jack said.

His father gave a curt nod.

"It was nice to meet you," Rachel stated with one of her signature smiles that could warm anyone's cold heart.

Logan actually cracked a grin. "You as well."

Jack turned and placed his hand on the small of Rachel's back as he led her out the door. The moment they were both in the car, tension surrounded them. The unspoken words, the obvious worry and the end of a happy evening all seemed to settle right between them.

"Well, that didn't go too bad."

Rachel's words sliced through the quiet, and Jack gripped the wheel as he pulled out of the drive. He couldn't argue with her, knowing that brief meeting could've been a whole lot worse.

"You didn't have to stand up for me," he stated. "I can handle my father."

"Oh…I just…"

Jack turned into Four Sisters a few moments later, frustrated at the man he'd become after just a few moments in the presence of his father.

"I didn't mean to sound ungrateful," he amended. "I appreciate what you're trying to do, but Dad doesn't always play nice. He wouldn't care if I sold the land to a developer who planned to tear it down and make a mall out of the property."

Rachel's gasp filled the vehicle. "Are you serious? That would be… Well, that would be horrendous. I'm starting to see why you seem so relaxed here and why you need a break."

Yes. Jack was starting to see those same things. Yet he'd worked so hard to have his own company under the umbrella of Hart Realty. An already established firm and a dynasty from his father that someday Jack could pass to his own children was all he'd ever wanted.

But Rosewood Valley calmed him, and he couldn't describe it, but he felt like home here.

"I just need to talk to him on my own." Jack pulled the car to a stop and glanced her way. "Sorry this night didn't end as nice as it started."

"No worries. Hope you and your dad have a nice talk." Rachel blinked and looked away as she reached for the handle. "I'll see you tomorrow, and we can work more on those built-ins. Good night, Jack."

She stepped from the car and Jack thought for certain her voice had cracked on those final words. Had he also seen a shimmer of unshed tears in her eyes before she stepped away?

Had he upset her with his gruff reply a moment ago? Or was she upset that she thought her own dream of the farm was slipping away? Either way, he didn't like this sinking feeling that he'd ruined the only bright spot in his life. The last thing he ever wanted was for Rachel to be hurt by anyone, most of all him. But now he had to go talk to his dad and hope Rachel wasn't too upset with him.

Rachel locked her door behind her as soon as she got into her loft apartment. She was going to grab a shower and head to bed. This evening had mentally drained her. Between the unexpected kiss that left her more hopeful than ever, to meeting Jack's father, to admitting Jack would be getting the home on the market soon, tonight's events had really torn into her emotions. She had to face the harsh reality that Jack was in charge of the farm and he had to sell it to appease his father and get that promotion. She couldn't ask him to keep waiting on her or try to give him less than it was worth. That wasn't fair because what if she was never in a financial spot to give him what the place was valued at?

There was a family out there who needed the land and the big house. A family who would love the place and care for it and fill the empty stalls with livestock. Rachel could still have her own farm someday; it just wouldn't be next door to her family. But she knew God would bless her in His time and not hers. She had to hold on to that.

Still. She was human and had feelings and a heart that hurt for what she thought she might obtain. Granted, Jack had never promised her anything. He'd been clear on what he needed to do, but she'd thought for certain they might be able to work something out.

Maybe she'd been too naive or too hopeful.

Right now, her head hurt and she just wanted to freshen up and put on her cozy pajamas.

As she made her way toward her room, her cat sprinted ahead of her. Clearly this was their new game. Her cell chimed from her pocket.

There went that sliver of hope again as she pulled it out thinking Jack had texted her.

But no. The message was from Walt in a group with her and Jack.

Can you both be at the store tomorrow at 8? I figured out who's been stealing. We're going to deal with it.

Well, at least this was something moving in the right direction. Rachel replied she'd be there and put her phone on her nightstand to charge. She didn't wait to see if Jack would reply. He was taking care of his own issues right now, and Rachel needed to spend her evening trying to relax and pray. She needed God more than ever now.

Chapter Seventeen

Jack had never felt so depleted and confused in his entire life. He'd barely slept for all the thoughts filling his mind. Lying in the darkness in his grandfather's home with all the memories to keep him company had really weighed on him last night. Those middle-of-the-night hours when there were no distractions and all he could do was think left Jack wondering what to do at this crossroads he now faced. Nobody could make this decision for him, and no matter what he decided, these next steps would be life-altering.

Rachel's truck was parked out back when he pulled up to the store, so he knew she'd beaten him here for this meeting. He hadn't spoken to her or texted since they parted ways last night. His last image of her was with those unshed tears in her eyes, and each time that thought pushed its way to the front of his mind, his heart clenched with a grip of guilt like he'd not ever experienced before.

He never wanted to hurt anyone, yet he'd done just that with his harsh reply and virtually stealing her dream right out from under her.

If he left town today and went back home, he'd have regrets for the rest of his life. Yet he'd still not come up with a solid answer. Even after discussing the ideas for the farm and timelines and price points, his father still had reservations and thought the land could go for more. When his father had broached the subject of the feed store, Jack circled back to the farm, not at all ready to discuss the store. Every part of him really felt like he wanted to keep this one piece of his grandfather. This final tie to the man who'd instilled these small-town values in him, and Jack had all the confidence that Walt would keep this place running while Jack was in San Francisco.

Jack made his way down the narrow hallway leading to the office. Chatter filtered from the open doorway and he recognized Walt's and Rachel's voices. Just that familiarity from her had his gut in knots. But he had to deal with whatever Walt found out first before he could deal with his own problems.

"Morning," Walt greeted him as soon as Jack stepped through the doorway.

Jack nodded his greeting, then turned a quick glance to do the same to Rachel. Her forced smile was all the proof he needed that he'd messed up.

"I figured having you both here would be best," Walt started, clearly oblivious to the tension. "I put in a small camera behind the counter the day Jack and I talked about the missing funds. Since then, I've seen a few instances with the same person and it's quite disheartening."

"Who is it?" Rachel asked.

"Myles."

Jack pulled in a deep breath and sighed. "I was hoping there would be some mistake or explanation. I hate having to fire someone so young."

"Maybe we don't have to fire him," Rachel chimed in. "I mean, we don't know the story."

Jack jerked his focus to her. "Not fire him? We can't have a thief working here."

"We don't know his side of things yet," she defended.

"Which is why I asked him to meet us this morning," Walt added. "He should be here any minute."

Rachel nodded and looked back at Walt. "I just don't want him to feel like we're attacking him."

"We're not attacking," Jack stated. "We're firing."

"Careful," Rachel muttered with a side-eye. "Your father is coming out."

Shocked at her reply, Jack could only stare as she completely turned her attention to Walt. Maybe his father was coming out in him, but stealing was stealing. How could there be a defense to that?

The chime on the back door cut through the strain in the room and the soft echo of footsteps filled the space.

Jack shifted aside to make room for Myles. The office wasn't big by any means, but add in four people and an awkward situation and things were going to be quite uncomfortable for a bit.

The moment Myles filled the doorway, his eyes took in the group and his jaw clenched.

"I'm in trouble." He remained in the doorway, but his shoulders dropped and his head hung just a bit more. "Did you call the cops or can I explain?"

Clearly the boy knew why they were all here. He wasn't stupid and had to have known he'd get caught at some point.

"Come on in, son," Walt invited. "We're not the firing squad."

Myles took one step in and stopped. He glanced around the room again and shoved his hands in his pockets.

"I want to hear why you took the money," Rachel told him. "We need to hear your reasoning. You were given a job and one that Walt trusted you with."

"I know."

The teen's head hung just a bit more, but Rachel's compassionate gaze never left the boy. Jack was having a difficult time focusing on anything or anyone else but her. He wanted a redo of last night, and he wanted to be alone with her to apologize. He couldn't leave things the way they had.

"I never intended to steal," Myles said. "I was so thankful to get a job to help out at home. My dad left and my mom is recovering from her chemo. I just thought my paycheck would go further than it does and then that cash was there and I thought just this one time."

Myles closed his eyes and shook his head. "But that one time turned into more. I was the only one bringing in any money after Dad left and my mom can't work for a while. I didn't want my sister to have to quit her dance lessons and…"

His voice cracked as he trailed off. Jack didn't know what to say. He'd had no clue the boy faced such hardships at home and was handling his life the best way he thought he could. And all he wanted to do was step up and provide when nobody else could. How could Jack be furious with that? How could anyone with a heart not empathize with this young boy's situation to care for his sick mother and younger sister?

Rachel moved and instantly wrapped Myles in an embrace. Jack met Walt's eyes and the older man had a sheen of tears. Clearly they all felt bad for Myles, and honestly, Jack had never been put in a position like this before.

"It will be okay." Rachel comforted the teen, then eased back from their hug. "But you cannot steal anymore. If you want to keep working, we want you here, but no more stealing."

Myles wiped his damp cheeks and looked between Jack and Walt.

"You're not calling the cops or firing me?" he asked.

Walt looked to Jack for guidance, and Jack crossed his arms as he weighed the right words to say here. This would be a pivotal point in this young boy's life, and Jack knew the final decision would be up to him.

"You're not fired and you're not going to see any cops," Jack confirmed. "But Rachel is right. You can't take any more money or we will have to take action."

Myles met his gaze. "I promise. You have my word."

Rachel's eyes darted to Jack, then back to Myles. "Why didn't you tell anyone you needed help?" she asked.

The boy shrugged and glanced away as if he had to protect his pride. "It's embarrassing, honestly. I never thought my parents would split up, especially while my mom was so sick. I left the football team so I could work, but I told everyone that I was tired of playing because I didn't want to explain myself."

Jack couldn't even imagine the heaviness this teen had been carrying around for months.

"Here's what I'd like to do if you and your family are okay with it," Rachel chimed in. "I'd like to host a fundraiser at Four Sisters. We do so many farm-to-table events, and I can't think of a better cause."

Myles blinked back more tears. "You'd do that for us?"

"Absolutely," she confirmed with that soft smile of hers that could bring peace to anyone's soul. "Sometimes you just have to ask for help. You have such a wonderful community. Anyone would rally around you guys, and there's absolutely nothing to be ashamed of."

Jack knew for a fact that if Rachel had known just how

dire this situation was, she would have intervened long before now. She truly had a heart for giving and loving.

She deserved nothing less in return.

"I thought I could do it all for them," Myles stated as he squared his shoulders and composed himself. "But it's been hard. I don't want my mom to be angry with me or disappointed, and you can take what I stole from my wages."

"Consider that a donation from the store," Jack stated before thinking of his reply. But now that the words were out, he was pleased with his answer. "We would have helped anyway had we known. But next time you need help, whether you work here or you're out in life, don't be afraid to tell someone. You'll find for the most part people are generous and willing to step up. You never know—you might be in a position one day when someone asks you for help and you'll be able to return the gesture."

Rachel's eyes met his and she gave a soft nod, silently approving everything he'd just said. He didn't know why, but he wanted to have her approval. To know he was making the right decision. And she'd been right to have patience with Myles and find out his side of the story before jumping straight to removing him from the workplace.

She'd also been right when she'd said his father was coming out in him. That was nearly all he knew—business and money. The low percentage of compassion and tenderness inside him came from his grandfather—and now he'd like to think from Rachel. She brought out that side of him, the side that had been buried by years of hustle and grinding in the city, trying to obtain that next level of success.

But there was so much more out there than money and success. There were feelings and real-life problems that required attention. If he was solely focused on himself and his next career move, how was he helping others?

"Your mother does need to know everything."

Walt's words cut through the room, and Jack nodded in agreement. "We will explain to her that you were only trying to help and that you're not going to be in trouble with us, so long as this is an isolated incident."

"I promise if you give me another chance, I will not do anything to betray you again," Myles insisted. "I need this job. Please."

"You can stay," Walt confirmed. "I'll call your mother later and have a talk with her and make sure she's not upset with you. I've known your family a long time, and I know your heart was in the right place."

"Thank you guys, so much."

Myles went around the room and hugged each one of them. "Can I still work this evening for my regular shift?"

"Absolutely." Walt nodded. "We need you here."

"I can't thank you enough for understanding. This is so embarrassing and—"

"You have no reason to be embarrassed for just trying to help your family," Rachel all but scolded. "I think you've learned your lesson, and I think you're going to grow from this."

"I've definitely learned my lesson and I can't thank you all enough for showing me grace."

Jack knew that was all Rachel. If he'd been in charge, he would've gone in leading with anger, while she went in leading with love. He could learn, and had learned, so much from her.

Once Myles left, Rachel also excused herself, leaving Jack and Walt alone.

"That went better than I thought it would," Walt stated as he sank back into his creaky old chair.

Jack nodded in agreement. "Let me know what his

mother says. And I'm going to think of other ways we can help. That poor boy has too much responsibility when he should be enjoying his last year of high school."

"We'll figure out something for the family," Walt said. "We can do a silent auction or have something here at the store after hours as well. We'll put our heads together and come up with something."

And that was why Jack loved this town. He'd yet to meet one selfish person. Everyone was constantly looking out for others, which was what life should be about, right?

The more these thoughts rolled around in his head, the more he wondered if God was speaking to him through a variety of outlets. All Jack had to do was be silent and listen.

Chapter Eighteen

Rachel stepped into the barn and glanced around for her father. Odd that he wasn't there, but that gave her a minute to send off a group text to her mother and sisters explaining the upcoming event she wanted to have to benefit Myles's family.

Once she was done, she shoved her cell into her back pocket and figured she might as well clean out the stalls. She wasn't sure what her father had planned for the day, but stalls always needed freshening up to keep the horses healthy.

Rachel adjusted her hat as she turned to grab a pitchfork but stopped short. Jack stood in the doorway. Hands in his pockets, in no hurry to speak or move inside, he just stood there.

"Are you trying to decide if you're staying or running?" she asked, also not moving any closer.

"We need to talk."

Rachel crossed her arms but said nothing. If he wanted the floor, she'd let him have it. But she had a feeling she wasn't going to like what he was about to say.

"I'm going back to San Francisco," he started, his words coming out slowly, as if he didn't want to be saying them at all. "My father left this morning."

Her heart started to break, but she had to remain strong. She knew from the beginning he wasn't going to stay.

"Short trip for him," she replied.

Jack shrugged. "He came for what he wanted and needed to get back to work."

"And is that what you are doing?" she asked. "Getting back to work before the farm is done?"

"I trust the contractors and I'll be back to see the final product and get it on the market. I'll pay you to finish those built-ins we started or I can have the guys do it."

"I'll finish it."

She didn't know why she agreed to that, because the only outcome from that project would be a reminder of something they'd started and couldn't finish…like the relationship she'd so hoped they'd have together.

"I'll make sure to compensate you for the time, especially now that I realize how tedious it is," he stated.

Rachel nodded, not quite sure what to say now. Whatever he and his father discussed last night had clearly thrust Jack back into mogul mode, and whatever she and Jack had shared was gone. Her heart sank realizing that in less than twenty-four hours, she'd lost any chance of every dream she'd ever had.

"Good for you," she replied. "I'm sure someone will be very happy there and love the changes you've made."

Jack nodded. "The new owner will love it, I'm certain. I just didn't want to leave town without telling you I'm sorry for last night."

"The kiss or the ending?"

He took a step forward but stopped. "The ending. I never intended to hurt you, Rachel. I hope you know that."

She kept her arms crossed for fear if she dropped them, he'd either see her hands shaking or she'd try to reach for him. She had to remain strong. She'd been through this before, right?

Well, they weren't exactly dating or engaged, but did it matter the label once the heart got so involved? She'd gone into this with her eyes wide open… Unfortunately her heart had been wide open as well, even though she'd tried her hardest to keep it closed.

"I believe you," she replied. "You were nothing but honest with me. God has other plans than what I wanted, and I'm sure it's something better than I ever could have imagined."

He opened his mouth but closed it and shook his head. She had no idea what he'd been about to say or what was truly on his heart. There wasn't a doubt in her mind that he was indeed sorry. Jack had a good heart; she'd seen it over and over. He wanted to do right by his grandfather and his father, and he felt torn. The two most influential men in his life were of two very different personalities and it was no wonder Jack was so conflicted.

"I feel foolish for asking, but can you keep on at the store for a bit and help Myles?"

There was that big heart she'd come to know and love. Even with all he had going on in his life right now, he still wanted to look out for those in need. How could she not be in love with him? But how could he be the one who felt so right and the one she thought should be in her life and still not fit in? Did he not feel the same? Did he not have any emotions after that kiss they'd shared?

"I'll be sure to keep Myles on my priority list," she assured him. "So you're keeping the store?"

Jack nodded. "For now. The farm is going to be my focus and then we'll see where life leads."

Would that path ever lead him back here for good? Or

would he just pop in and out—or worse, call or text to keep tabs on the feed store from afar? She had a sinking feeling that once he got back into his element, he'd forget all about Rosewood Valley…and about her.

"Well, thanks for letting me know."

She really needed him to go so she could have a good, healthy cry while mucking stalls.

"If there's nothing else, I really need to get to work," she told him when he simply continued to stand there as if he wanted to say more.

When the silence became too much and he still remained standing, that bold mouth of hers took over. Her words spilled out before her mind could tell her to stop.

"Did that kiss mean nothing?" she asked. "Was that a spur-of-the-moment reaction?"

"It meant something." His soft tone only caused her heart to crack more.

"I don't know why I let myself think you had changed since you arrived," she murmured, unable to stop her thoughts from spilling out. "I thought there was more between us, that maybe you would consider staying. I know you promised nothing—in fact, you were quite honest about your plans and I didn't want to face the truth."

Yet again, Jack opened his mouth, then closed it. Whatever his response was, he clearly had more self-control than she did.

She so wished he'd say something, though. Like maybe he'd fallen for her and they could try this long-distance thing or that he'd come back and try to give them a chance.

But he merely nodded.

"Thanks for everything. You don't know the impact you've had on my life and how I wish things were different right now."

Before she could ask him what he meant, Jack turned on his booted heel and walked out.

She realized for the first time he had on the boots she'd given him. Clearly she *had* left an impression on his life, and maybe she would be hard to forget.

The moment tires crunched over the gravel in the drive, Rachel blew out a breath and pulled off her hat. She curled the brim between her fingers and closed her eyes, trying to block out the additional hurt that threatened to creep in.

"I take it you and Jack are no longer a thing, from the way he tore out of here?"

Rachel jerked her head up to see her father striding toward her with a concerned look on his face.

She couldn't speak as emotions clogged her throat. Rachel closed the distance and thrust herself into her father's open arms. The moment he embraced her, she used his strong shoulder to pour her sadness onto. She knew he'd always be there for her, just like she knew she'd get through this. But sometimes, a girl just needed a hug from her dad.

Jack pulled in front of the office he'd called his home away from home for nearly his entire adult life. As he stared up at the black-and-white sign above the double doors, the words HART REALTY stared back at him.

How many times over the years had he walked beneath that and taken this for granted? More importantly, how many times had *he* himself been taken for granted?

Far too many to count, in his opinion.

Jack glanced down to his boots and a ball of dread curled in his stomach as a lump formed in his throat.

Yeah, he knew where he was most appreciated. Leaving Rosewood Valley had been one of the most difficult decisions he'd ever made, but he'd known all along he belonged back here, where his job and his home were. He couldn't abandon his goals now. Not when he'd worked so hard and for so long to see them come true.

Or could he? Since leaving yesterday, he'd felt nothing but worry and anxiety and a healthy dose of guilt. When he'd first arrived in Rosewood Valley, he felt confident that when he finished his business there and returned to San Francisco, he would be elated and ready to take that promotion he knew should go to him.

Yet the whole drive back home, all Jack could think about was Rachel and her parting words. The sadness in her voice, the unshed tears she'd so desperately tried to hide. He'd only wanted to bring her joy and happiness like she'd done to him, but he'd broken her heart.

And he hadn't lied. Their kiss *had* meant something. In the short amount of time he'd been with her, his entire life had changed, and he could honestly say he was a better man for it.

So if he noticed that much of a difference in just a few weeks, what would happen if he spent a lifetime with her?

Jack had no idea why he was thinking long-term with Rachel, but the idea didn't scare him. In fact, for the first time since leaving, he had a burst of hope and a positive outlook on his future. While he had no clue what that looked like right now, he knew who he wanted in his life.

Jack took the steps leading to the doors and let himself in. The modern design of metal and leather with black accents was a far cry from the country life he'd been living. Walking back in here now, the office seemed almost… sterile. There were no pops of color, no flowers, nothing cozy at all.

His father stepped from the back, where the coffee bar was tucked into a small nook.

"Son. What are you doing back?" he asked, holding a black mug with the company logo on the side. "I thought you were seeing the project through to the sale."

Jack eyed the row of clear tables with industrial legs that lined either side of the room. There were enough desk areas for eight Realtors and each one had an occupant that would be in later. Thankfully they were alone as Jack moved toward his workspace. He eyed the photo on the edge of the desk, the one where he stood in front of the first home he'd ever sold. He always wanted that reminder, but the main thing he remembered was that his father hadn't been there that day. He'd been at another listing and said he couldn't make the open house where Jack had finally sealed his first deal.

"I plan on seeing the farm renovation through completely," he stated, glancing back up to his father. "I needed to come here and settle a few things first."

"I didn't see that you had a closing scheduled today."

"I meant business with you."

His father's brows rose slightly, and for the first time Jack could recall, Logan Hart was speechless and surprised.

"If this is about the promotion—"

"It is," Jack confirmed.

"You know it's all going to depend on the sale," his father told him, then took another sip of his coffee. "Brian has quite a bit in the works and has already made some great progress working out of the new office to get a jump start before our official grand opening."

"Good for him." Hearing this didn't bother Jack, and he realized he wasn't jealous of Brian and didn't want to one-up him to get that office for himself. "I'm taking myself out of the running for the promotion."

The coffee cup lowered slowly as his father's gaze narrowed. "Excuse me?"

Just admitting those words out loud lifted a weight from Jack's shoulders. He couldn't imagine how he'd feel once he put his thoughts into actions. The chains were breaking, and he had one family and one town to thank for opening his eyes.

He also had to thank God. Those prayers hadn't gone unnoticed or unanswered. Jack simply had to be open to God's plan.

"I've been praying and doing quite a bit of calculating in my head, especially on my drive here. At this time in my life, I'm going to step away from San Francisco and from Hart Realty."

His father set his mug on the closest desk and propped his hands on his hips, never once breaking eye contact with Jack. Jack knew this conversation wouldn't be well received, but it was long overdue.

"What did that woman do to you?" his father demanded.

Instead of being angry or defensive as he probably would've been in the past, Jack merely smiled when he thought of Rachel.

"She showed me there's more than money and there's more than working all the time," he replied. "There's family and peace and a laid-back way of living I didn't know existed. I mean, I experienced it as a child when I would visit Grandpa, but to embrace that culture as an adult is a different story."

"You're just like him," Jack's father muttered. "My dad never could understand why I was here in the city, never understood why I ever wanted to leave Rosewood Valley. But once I went to college, I knew I'd never live in that small town again. I needed people and the hustle I could only find here."

"And that's what works for you and makes you happy," Jack replied. "That's what works for Brian, and I thought that's what worked for me. I see things so much differently now. There's a calm inside of me that's been brought to the surface, and I don't recall being happier."

Well, if he didn't completely mess things up with Rachel. He wanted to go back and tell her how he felt, but he had to settle all of this first. He wanted a clean slate and nothing in his way once he presented his future to her.

"I thought I'd lose you," his father admitted, blowing out a sigh. "I've been hard on you because I wanted you to always be here with me. I wanted us to be a team, and I thought if I made you work harder day after day, you'd take over the company. But I've always known you were more like my father than I ever was."

Jack wasn't sure if this was his father's attempt at an apology, but the man seemed almost tired. Like he'd been waiting for this moment to come and now he could breathe.

"I don't resign to hurt you." Jack needed him to know that above all else. "The city is not for me anymore, and if Brian wants to take over, then he should. He's great at what he does."

"So are you," his father retorted. "So what will you do in the country? I'm not sure you're knowledgeable enough about farm life."

Jack laughed and shook his head, loving the way this conversation had turned. His dad seemed understanding, which completely caught Jack off guard in the best way.

"I actually thought about still doing real estate and maybe opening my own office there. You're right, and I am good at what I do."

"Would you use the Hart name?" his father asked, reaching for his mug once again.

Jack blinked, surprised at the question. "I didn't think I would. I mean, you have two offices here in the city and Rosewood Valley is hours away."

"Doesn't mean we can't have another office and one that you deserve to run."

Never in Jack's dreams had he thought his father would offer another branch, but his father likely had never considered another town outside the city. Maybe they could still continue to work together, to keep their bond, and perhaps Jack could show his dad some grace and pull him around to seeing that there was so much more than just a top-dollar sale.

"I admit, this isn't how I thought our talk would go," Jack stated, circling the desk to get closer to his dad. "I thought you'd be angry and push back about my decision."

Logan merely shrugged. "I'm not thrilled you're leaving, and I never understood the draw for that slow-paced lifestyle, but I guess there's something for everyone. And if we can tap into that market, then that's a good thing."

Of course they circled back to money. If Jack was going to use the Hart name and open another branch, there had to be some ground rules set in place first.

"Rosewood Valley is quite a different demographic than San Francisco," Jack explained. "If I use the Hart name under our umbrella, then I'll be running the office how I see fit and I have final say."

His father merely studied him as if weighing the proposal. Jack crossed his arms once again, determined to stand his ground. He could open a space on his own. He wouldn't need to use the company at all, but having his father's support would make a difference. He knew without a doubt he could make a go of things on his own. This was what he knew, what he was good at, and how he could provide for Rachel. He didn't want money to be the driving factor, not like his dad did.

Ultimately, his father nodded. "I would trust you to start up an office within the company. I think you lead more with your heart, and from what I can tell, that's how business is done in that small town. They'll probably love you for it."

Jack hoped. He didn't have an office space and he didn't have anything in place other than the seed planted in his head. But he knew just like with this initial decision, once he prayed over it, God would lead him to the right place and be with him the entire way. Jack only hoped Rachel would be at his side.

"I won't exclude you from business dealings, and I'll make sure the line of communication is always open," Jack added, taking another step toward his father. "We can have our attorney draw up any documents and get this next chapter started. I just truly feel my home is in Rosewood Valley."

Logan nodded. "You seem at peace right now."

Jack couldn't recall the last time he'd had a sense of calm wash over him and through him. He wanted to rush headfirst into this next phase, but he had to take his time and make sure each stone was set in place before taking that next unknown step.

"I'm proud of you, son."

His father's words jerked Jack's focus back. "You are?"

He nodded, put the cup down again and reached for Jack. As he pulled him into a firm embrace, Jack welcomed the love his father rarely showed. Jack didn't think the man knew how to show too much emotion, but deep in his heart, Jack knew his father did love him. This display of emotions no doubt had Logan Hart feeling vulnerable and out of his comfort zone, but Jack would remember this moment forever.

"You're stronger than I ever was," his father stated with a firm pat on the back before easing away. "You want that balance of family and career, and I believe you will pull it off. I'm afraid I put career above all else because I tried to compensate for your mother being gone. I thrust myself into work to ignore the pain, and at times I forgot how to be a father."

Jack stared back into his father's dark brown eyes, noting the fine wrinkles fanning from the corners. They'd both suffered when Jack's mom passed, and he hadn't known how much his father hurt. He always attributed his father working to uncaring emotions, but clearly it was the opposite. Logan Hart had tried to push away his pain, to mask it, by keeping busy and ignoring reality.

"About my penthouse here," Jack started. "I'll be putting it on the market as soon as possible."

"And you'll be living at Circle H, I presume?"

Jack smiled. "I can't think of anywhere else I'd rather be. I'd love for you to come visit. I'll keep a room ready for you at all times."

"I'd like that," his father stated with a smile that reached his dark eyes. "What about Rachel?"

His heart soared at the mention of her name. "I'll be asking her to marry me."

His father blinked. "Already? Are you sure she's the one?"

"I'm as sure of that as I am about this move." He'd never been more positive of any other decision in his life. "This is right for me, Dad."

"Then I can't wait to get to know her more. She's really changed you, and as much as I hate to see you go, I'm glad to see you so happy."

Jack gave his father one more embrace, feeling like maybe they'd turned over a new chapter in their family life as well. Full of hope and love, Jack had a feeling his entire world was just about to begin.

Chapter Nineteen

A utopilot.

Rachel had heard that term over the years, but she'd never fully understood the concept until now. For the past several days, she'd been working at the farm, at the store, on her schooling, and trying to organize a fundraiser for Myles and his family. But staying busy had kept her mind off a certain someone. Not that it had helped. Thoughts of Jack continually rolled through her mind, and she wondered what he was doing. He'd been gone for what seemed like forever, but in reality, it had been four days.

She'd pulled her cell out countless times to text him, but what would she say? She certainly didn't want to look desperate or clingy; she just genuinely missed him. She was a bit surprised he hadn't reached out to check on anything, but maybe once he hit the city, he'd opted to go into full work mode.

Rachel made her way toward her barn and barely had enough energy to climb those stairs. She'd put in ten hours on the farm and four at the store. One of these days, when she got her new home, she would make sure there was a large soaker tub for days like today. For now, she'd have to settle for a hot shower to ease her sore muscles.

Maybe some hot tea would help, too. She'd add some local honey for a bit of sweetness. Maybe she'd try to find a new book, curl up on her sofa with a thick blanket and her cat, and attempt to get lost in a fictitious world where everyone got a happy ending.

The moment Rachel pushed her door open, she stilled. Her eyes landed right on the most obscene bouquet of flowers in a vase on her kitchen table. She glanced around and found Jack sitting on the sofa with the cat in his lap.

"We've become friends," he stated, stroking his fingertips between the cat's ears.

Rachel stepped inside and closed the door behind her, shutting out the cool fall evening air. "What are you doing here?"

He remained unmoving while he continued to pet the cat. How could he be so casual like he wasn't affected by being here again? Her heart beat much too fast, and she wished she'd had some heads-up that he was here.

"I didn't see your car," she mentioned.

"I hid it around back so I could surprise you."

He'd definitely done just that.

"And did you bring in this arrangement?" she asked, moving to the table. "I've never seen such a variety, and it's nearly as large as the table."

She couldn't help but laugh the more she looked at it. "I mean, thank you, but why all these flowers?"

Jack carefully lifted the cat and sat him on the couch cushion next to him before standing. "I figured you put an arrangement in my house—it's only fitting I return the gesture."

The wound to Rachel's heart healed just a bit as hope smoothed over her like a balm. She didn't want to get her hopes up or assume, but the fact he came back sooner than he'd mentioned did make her wonder.

"I'm not as good as you with flower arrangements, so I

admit I paid for that." He chuckled, sliding his hands into his pockets.

"It's perfect." She reached to touch one buttery-soft pale pink petal. Then her eyes landed on something. "Is that a card?"

"Is there a card tucked in there?" he asked. "Hmm. See what it says."

She eyed him, but he gave no clue as to what he was thinking or that he even knew a card had been placed there. Either he was a good actor or he truly had no idea the florist had put a message inside all these stems.

Rachel pulled the white card from the bouquet and started reading. She didn't get far before her heart clenched and her eyes started watering. She blinked away the moisture and started over so she could take it all in at once.

Rachel, I want to start a new life with you. I want to make the Circle H our home.

I want to marry you if you'll have me.

When Rachel looked back to Jack, he was on one knee holding a velvet box, and her stomach curled into knots as her heart leaped to her throat.

"I might have taken a couple wrong turns in life," he started. "But I can't be upset about any of them since they all led me here and to falling in love with you."

Too many emotions clogged Rachel's throat. She couldn't believe this moment was happening. Having Jack here proposing went far beyond anything she'd ever hoped or dreamed of.

She swallowed. "When I didn't hear from you at all,

I thought you just shifted back to work mode and forgot all about this place."

"You're kidding, right? I could never forget the farm that shaped me or the woman who opened my eyes to faith and love. I belong here, and I'm hoping you'll give me an answer soon because my knee is hurting."

Rachel laughed and nodded. "Yes, of course I will marry you."

"You haven't seen the ring yet." He lifted the lid as he came to his feet. "What if you don't like it?"

"I don't even need a ring. I just need you."

When he pulled the ring from the box, she stared down at the simple round stone in a gold band. Nothing fancy, but delicate and absolutely perfect.

"This was my grandmother's," he explained. "And if you want something different, we can go pick it out—"

"No. This is the ring I want."

She didn't know what she loved more, the fact he had his grandmother's ring or that his hands were shaking as he slid the band onto her finger. Clearly she wasn't the only one with nerves here.

"You know I'm not a flashy girl," Rachel went on, admiring how perfectly the ring fit and looked on her hand. "With all the work I do, this ring couldn't be more perfect. I hope your grandmother would've liked me."

Jack gave her hand a soft squeeze. "I don't remember too much about her, but I don't know how anyone couldn't fall in love with you. I did in record time, and I know my grandfather adored your family. I imagine he's smiling down right now on both of us."

Rachel hadn't known such a level of happiness existed. She hadn't known that God's ultimate plan far exceeded anything she could have ever planned for herself. All she'd had to do was wait and trust in His timing.

"I have no doubt your grandparents are proud of the man you've become and that you'll be living on the farm to start the next generation."

How had their vastly different dreams turned into the same one? To know she'd be getting each dream she'd ever prayed for while honoring the memory of Jack's grandparents absolutely made Rachel more fulfilled than she could have ever imagined. Her family would be so thrilled for them, and she couldn't wait to tell them everything. But for now she just wanted to enjoy her time with Jack and discuss all the plans and dream of their life together.

"What did your dad say?" she asked. "I assume you told him."

Jack sighed but continued to hold on to her hand. "I told him and at first he was hesitant, but then he said he knew I was heading in this direction. He's happy for us."

"Really?" Both shock and elation filled her. "That's great. I'm sure you were nervous for that talk."

He took her hand and led her to the couch. Once he took a seat, she sank next to him and curled her feet to her side as she leaned into him.

"I was, but I was more nervous about the idea of not coming back here and taking over the farm and asking you to marry me." He took her hand and covered it on his lap. "I had to get some things in order before I came back, so that's why I wasn't in touch. I didn't want to waste a minute. I put my penthouse on the market and I've already had some interest."

"That's wonderful," she stated.

He offered her one of those grins that never failed to make her heart flip. "I plan on using that money to help Myles with his family, if that's okay with you."

There went another flip. "More than okay, but you don't have to run that by me."

He toyed with the stone on her ring as he held her gaze. "I do. We're a team now."

"I think they will be grateful, and your heart is so big. It's no wonder I fell in love with you."

That grin turned into a beaming smile. "You love me?"

Rachel jerked back slightly. "Of course I love you. I wouldn't have agreed to marry you if I didn't."

"I just hadn't heard you say it."

She rested her head on his shoulder and laced their fingers together. "I can't wait to say it every single day for the rest of my life."

"I look forward to that. There's also another part of my plan that I need to discuss with you."

Rachel lifted her head and narrowed her eyes. "You've been doing quite a bit of soul-searching since you left here."

"Praying," he corrected. "And I was doing plenty of it while I was here, but I wanted to make sure I had my old life in order before I came to you asking for a new life together."

Wow. She knew nobody was perfect, but she couldn't help but think God had created the perfect mate just for her.

"So what's the other part of your plan? I hope it involves buying a hat if you're going to live on a farm."

His laughter rumbled against her, filling her with more love and adoration.

"We can go hat shopping anytime you want," he confirmed. "But I plan on opening a real estate firm here if you're okay with that."

"Okay with that? I think that's a great idea. You're good at what you do, and people will love having George Hart's grandson selling them homes."

"I hope so. I want to provide for you the way you deserve."

Rachel swatted at his chest. "I don't need you to provide for me. We're in this together, remember? We'll take care of each other, and I have total faith in you that you will do amazing."

"I suppose we need to get some animals," he suggested. "I have no clue on that, so it's definitely your call."

"First, we're getting you a horse."

He held her tighter against his side. "I can get on board with that. But I think our first order of business is to talk to your family. How do you think they'll receive this?"

Rachel could already imagine the hugs from her sisters and mom and how thrilled her father would be that the adjoining farm would be part of their family from now until forever.

"They will love every bit of this," she assured him. "How soon can we get married?"

Jack laughed once again and held her close as the cat jumped onto his lap and walked across to hers.

"In a hurry?" he asked.

"I just want to start our forever," she said.

He tipped her chin up and stared into her eyes. "Our forever started the moment you rode up on your horse and professed your childhood crush."

When he laid his lips softly on hers, she knew in her heart she had followed God's path and waited for the one. There was no doubt in her mind that she and Jack would have a beautiful life together and she would thank God in every one of her prayers for this blessing and all those to come.

* * * * *

*If you enjoyed this story,
be sure to check out*

A Cowgirl's Homecoming

*the first book in the delightful
Four Sisters Ranch series
by Julia Ruth!*

Available now from Love Inspired.

Discover more at LoveInspired.com.

Dear Reader,

Welcome back to Rosewood Valley! I hope you are loving the Four Sisters Ranch series. The next sister we visited was Rachel. This no-nonsense, loyal rancher had huge goals and had prayed for a farm, and family, of her own. When the farm next door was up for sale, she truly believed this was the door God had opened for her. There was just one minor problem…

Jack Hart had his own goals and selling this inheritance was number one. He had no use for a farm in the middle of this nowhere town. But turning this home into a profit only stirred up memories from his childhood, and Rachel, along with her family, helped him realize there was so much more to life than money. And that sometimes the best-laid plans aren't your own.

I hope you enjoyed this installment from Rosewood Valley and fell in love with this quaint town and all of the characters. Jack and Rachel were so fun to write as their story unfolded and their faith grew. If you are new to Four Sisters, please go back and pick up *A Cowgirl's Homecoming*, to read about Jenn and Luke.

Happy Reading,
Julia